M.M.

Milrose Munce

DOUGLAS ANTHONY COOPER

and the Den of
Professional
Help

DOUBLEDAY CANADA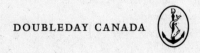

Doubleday Canada and colophon are trademarks.

Library and Archives Canada Cataloguing in Publication

Cooper, Douglas, 1960-
Milrose Munce and the den of professional help / Douglas
Anthony Cooper.

ISBN: 978-0-385-66080-8
PAPERBACK ISBN: 978-0-385-66081-5

I. Title.

PS8555.O59195M54 2007   jC813'.54   C2006-906346-X

Cover illustration: Anita Johnston
Printed and bound in the USA

Published in Canada by
Doubleday Canada, a division of
Random House of Canada Limited

Visit Random House of Canada Limited's website:
www.randomhouse.ca

BVG   10   9   8   7   6   5   4   3   2   1

Dedicated,
with appropriate solemnity,
to Elly Belly

THE FIRST DUTY IN LIFE IS TO BE AS
ARTIFICIAL AS POSSIBLE. WHAT THE SECOND
DUTY IS NO ONE HAS AS YET DISCOVERED.
—*Oscar Wilde*

CHAPTER
ONE

MILROSE MUNCE WAS ON FINE TERMS WITH
THE DEAD. SOME OF HIS BEST FRIENDS WERE,
IN FACT, LONG DECEASED. THEY WERE MAGNIF-
ICENTLY REPULSIVE, AND DID THEIR BEST TO
KEEP HIM ENTERTAINED.

Milrose did sometimes wonder whether his
school produced more dead students than the average. Perhaps it did. On the other hand, adolescence
was hilariously perilous on the whole, and it was a
wonder those idyllic years failed to claim even more
lives. Milrose himself was lucky to have survived
numerous death-defying acts of everyday youth. So
perhaps other schools were equally stuffed with vile
wandering ghosts. It would also make sense if this
were not a well-known fact—Milrose could imagine
the staff doing their best not to emphasize fatality

rates in meetings with parents. Certainly, precise figures regarding the prematurely departed never seemed to make it into the brochures.

Not that Milrose Munce was the least distressed by the impressive population of hideous wraiths in his own school. Life would be so much less interesting without death.

Milrose was on especially fine terms with the disgusting apparitions on the third floor. Other floors were less friendly, true: the ghouls in the school basement, for instance, were a touch wary of him. Milrose sympathized. He knew that his mere presence served to make them feel inadequate and uncomfortable. Milrose Munce was, you see—through no fault of his own—intelligent. Basement ghouls, who liked to lurk in lockers, were generally athletes who had done something exceptionally stupid on the playing field and had died a gruesome death as a result. They were not always pleased to be confronted with a boy who was, unfairly, still alive at fifteen and who was—even worse—a dire athlete and not at all dense.

Milrose was not particularly well loved on the second floor, either. The ghosts on that floor were not precisely hostile, but they were just as full of themselves as dead athletes, and possibly even less talented. Milrose, who did not take many things very seriously (himself, especially), found these pompous phantoms unbearable.

Poisoned Percy was typical of the second-floor ghosts. Percy had died while attempting to fake suicide. He had hoped that this performance would make him famous as a poet: that once he were revived in hospital, the literary world would take his suffering seriously and recite his verses at funerals. In fact, the only funeral at which his poems were ever recited was his own, where the audience ground their teeth throughout the ceremony in an attempt not to grimace. The sound of grinding teeth occasionally drowned out the reader.

Percy, typically of the second floor, had no sense of humour regarding his life's unpleasant conclusion. He had been careful to leave a bottle marked "Poison Hemlock (*Conium maculatum*)" beside him, after swallowing pills secretly removed from an entirely different, less poisonous bottle marked "Vitamin C." No, he had never been the sort of boy to laugh at his own shortcomings, and when the pellets he dramatically swallowed turned out not to be Vitamin C but instead expensive first-class rat poison, he was deeply annoyed. His mother always felt kind of awful about her decision to store rodenticide in a vitamin bottle, but these things are not easy to remedy after the fact.

When Milrose encountered Percy, the pale poet would only sometimes condescend to take notice of the living boy. "Oh, Munce . . . there you are. How's life?"

Milrose would shrug. "Fine. How's death?"

"Droll, Munce."

Milrose insisted upon calling the ghost Percy, which was short for his given name, Percival. Percy insisted that his real name was Parsifal, but nobody believed him.

Yesterday, Milrose had run into Percy on the way to Math, and—against his better judgment—decided to chat. Being late for Math was something Milrose occasionally enjoyed, and yesterday had felt like the right kind of day to be irresponsible.

"So, you working on stuff that's fresh, Poisson?"

"Always. A poet is always working. Even when I sleep, I am at work. It is my whole being. I am now writing an epic poem, if you must know. It will be . . . epic."

"I forget. Does epic mean 'long,' or 'dull'? Or both?"

"It means deeply moving. And my theme in particular will move even the coarsest soul to tears."

"Even mine, huh." Milrose sighed. "Um, all right. What's the theme?"

"Digestion."

"What?"

"Digestion. And its enemy: indigestion. I'll read you what I have so far."

"Kind of busy today, Perce."

"It's only seventy-two pages. And the name's Parsifal."

"Decent of you to think of me. But I'm no critic. And I'm *really* busy, in fact."

Percy had removed a thick, ominous manuscript from his prissy school bag. While he was arranging the pages, however, and clearing his throat, the bell had rung.

"Sorry, Perce. Never been late for Math. Famous for it: never being late. Gotta run."

Percy barely had time to utter the words "The Flavour of Indigestion, An Epic Poem in Twelve Parts," before his victim had achieved safe haven in the stairwell.

The dear decayed on the third floor were nothing like the dull dead on the floors below. These were most often the victims of science experiments gone wrong, and they had a sense of humour regarding their untimely mistakes.

Cryogenic Kelvin, for example, had assumed that a cup of liquid nitrogen would make for a refreshing cool drink. His professor had been too busy dissecting a giant carnivorous slug to notice that Kelvin was turning an interesting shade of blue and was growing wet with condensation. When Kelvin began to emit a crackling noise, Professor Pointell finally noticed him. "Kelvin, you're not looking well. Why don't you take a seat."

Kelvin bent to sit down, and immediately shattered into ice cubes, which melted mournfully all over the floor.

Cryogenic Kelvin, dead and cheerful, had a good attitude towards his final mistake. "Yeah, well . . . it's because Caroline Corduroy broke my heart. I mean, she also broke my liver, my kidneys, my eyeballs, and my spleen. But whatever. I thought she was pretty hot." Kelvin would pause, like a professional comic. "Guess she found me kind of cold."

This joke was a riot the first time Milrose heard it. The next time it was a touch less riotous, and by the fourth time it was getting a bit stale. Still, Kelvin was a fine ex-fellow, even if his jokes were a bit repetitive and his eyes were frozen in their sockets and his skin was cadaverously pallid.

During biology class, these days, Kelvin would park himself beside the skeleton at the front of the room, his dead blue arm around its bony shoulders. Milrose was the only one who could see this; in fact, Milrose was fairly sure that no one else was even *aware* that the school was bulging with the posthumous.

"Why are you snorting, Milrose?" the teacher would ask him, suspiciously.

"Nervous habit, sir. Family thing. Can't be helped. My great-grandfather used to snort, even at funerals . . . tragic, really."

On a tedious Monday a few months back Kelvin had been particularly inspired. Yes, as always, he had stood for a minute with his arm around the skeleton. Yes, Milrose had snorted. Then, however—probably to see whether he could elicit something more poignant than a snort—Kelvin decided to take the skeleton dancing.

The class, who were uniformly bored, perked up to see the skeleton unhook itself from its glorified coat rack. Some of them more than perked up: ten giggled, fourteen squealed, six of them screamed, and the entire front row passed out.

Mr. Shorten knew full well that he was not the sort of teacher to make students squeal, scream, and faint. Giggle, yes. But Mr. Shorten was a dull teacher—he had always been dull—so he wondered what was the cause of all this excitement. He did not have to wonder long. For the skeleton wheeled gracefully into his vision, as if waltzing with an invisible partner. Which, of course, it *was*.

Milrose was impressed to note that Kelvin was a competent ballroom dancer. This was a side of his friend that he had not yet witnessed. He wondered whether Kelvin might also be able to tap dance, and whether he might be willing to give Milrose lessons. Milrose Munce had never had the slightest desire to become, say, a good soccer player, but he had always wanted to learn tap.

Mr. Shorten was not having anything like these casual thoughts. He in fact sympathized, greatly, with the front row of the class, and considered passing out cold himself.

"Stop that!" said Mr. Shorten, feebly, probably aware that he did not have much authority over a waltzing skeleton. And this proved correct, for the skeleton did not stop that at all.

The gigglers became squealers as the skeleton whirled daintily in their direction. The squealers screamed, and the screamers fainted. Milrose was thrilled at the escalating excitement. Now *this* was a performance.

When Kelvin and the skeleton had completed their magnificent tour, they returned to the steel mount. Before hanging the bones up and calling it a day, however, Kelvin arranged to have the skeleton perform a gracious curtsy: a truly revolting gesture.

Milrose Munce had provoked suspicion when he stood at the end of this spectacle to applaud loudly. It was noted. Nobody *else* had enjoyed the dance.

Mr. Shorten in particular looked very, very suspicious. This was not the first time he had experienced Milrose behaving in peculiar and inappropriate ways. For instance, just a couple of days before, Kelvin had been telling his Caroline Corduroy joke for the seventeenth time, and Milrose—though not enjoying it quite as much as the first, or even the twelfth time—

had made sure to laugh and slap his dead friend heartily on the back. (He was careful to remove his hand quickly, however, as warm skin would often stick to Kelvin, and frostbite was an issue.) Mr. Shorten had witnessed this: Milrose Munce giving a hearty slap on the back to someone who—as far as Shorten could determine—wasn't there.

The science teacher was not the only staff member who was beginning to take note of these peculiar incidents: how Milrose seemed to have a cheerful relationship with, well, empty space. Milrose, however, being carefree and irresponsible, had not taken note that note was being taken.

The other ghouls on the third floor were an equally fine group, and many could match Kelvin in terms of dramatic flair. Ghosts had a life of their own, which consisted mostly of not being alive: lazing about, telling stories. When Milrose joined them, however, they were often moved to dramatize these stories in sensational ways.

Stuck Stu, for instance, would masterfully re-enact his own sad demise: how he had accidentally jammed his thumb into an Erlenmeyer flask full of a complex substance that was on the verge of exploding.

After failing to rescue his thumb, Stu had politely addressed his fellow classmates: "Um, you guys, I think you better leave the room." And, acknowledging his situation, they had regretfully done just that.

After which the flask—and Stu with it—had exploded in a truly dazzling fashion, with pieces of both flask and Stu embedded so deeply in the walls and desks and blackboard that students even today were occasionally finding shards of glass or bone emerging sharply from odd places.

The moment of the re-enacted explosion itself was most fun to watch, as Stuck Stu would in fact explode (an easy enough thing for an unwhole ghost), so that multiple bloody bits of him would hang jiggling from objects all about the room.

After collecting himself, Stuck Stu would bow dramatically, to an enthusiastic ovation.

Deeply Damaged Dave was, next to Kelvin, Milrose Munce's closest friend among the dead. They had bonded in their mutual love of unstable chemicals: in particular, substances (like Stu) that could be made to explode in exciting ways. Dave, had his life not been cut woefully short, might have made a brilliant scientist, or criminal.

Dave's demise was a consequence of his desire to test the reputed powers of rubidium, a substance said to be capable of producing truly exquisite eruptions. This was not something students were encouraged to test in the school lab, so Dave—and this moral error cost him his life—had quietly put a glass ampoule of rubidium in his pocket, intending to do the experiment in the quiet of his own living room.

Rubidium does indeed explode in breathtaking fashion. And it is easy to set the stuff off: all you have to do is soak it in water. Which is why it was so very sad that Dave got caught in a torrential downpour on the way home from school with that stolen rubidium in his pocket. In his anger at becoming thoroughly soaked, Dave had punched himself in the hip—a peculiar but typical gesture, usually harmless, which in this case broke the glass ampoule. And the rest is, as they say, history. As was Dave.

Milrose was also fond of Toasted Theresa and Floating Phil, lovebirds who had died, as lovebirds do, within minutes of each other. What was peculiar—and adorable—was that both had died by accident, at opposite ends of the building, without either being aware of the other's passing: Theresa caught fire in the chemical storeroom, just as Phil was swallowing much of the pool.

And then there was Bored Beulah, who had fallen asleep and into a vat of hydrochloric acid. She was an amusing if deadpan ghoul. Beulah was not the sort to put on a show, but she was nevertheless entertaining, in a bored sort of way. "You're too lively for me, Milrose. You should learn to be cool. Study Kelvin. He's a cool dude."

Milrose had always suspected that Beulah's studied ennui was in truth a facade for a complex and probably fascinating personality, but he had never had any

success in piercing that surface. People who practise cool tend to be deeply shallow, but Beulah gave
the occasional indication of being very much the
opposite. It was the look she would give Milrose
sometimes, when he said something perceptive
(which he did more often than he recognized).
Beulah, although her own person was impenetrable,
seemed capable of seeing right to the hidden centre of
others—even people like Milrose, who still had flesh.

The dead were not entirely sure why Milrose could
see them. Ghosts are of course capable of making
themselves seen or heard by anyone—this is necessary in the ordinary process of haunting—but they
reserve this talent for special occasions. Even the
dimmest dead thing understands that if everyone
were haunted on a regular basis, it would reduce the
impact of the experience. In fact, ghosts generally
choose to reveal themselves only to people who do
not believe in ghosts. This tends to be the most effective way to inspire handsome hair-whitening panic.

After years of study, certain living humans can
learn to see ghosts—professional exorcists, for
instance. Milrose, however, had simply been born
with this peculiar capability. Some people can put a
leg behind their head; some can extend their tongue
halfway up a nostril; Milrose Munce could see ghosts.

Not that these ghosts were much to look at.
What little flesh Beulah retained, for instance, was

not *healthy* flesh. And Toasted Theresa was even less likely to win any beauty contests, as the chemical fire she had chosen to ignite had been impervious to fire extinguishers, and it had taken a couple of hours to put her out. Floating Phil was probably as fetching as any bloated corpse, but Deeply Damaged Dave was simply not enjoyable to look at; after all, he had damaged such an intimate and necessary part of his person. Milrose did not require his friends to be all that good looking, though, and he had quickly grown accustomed to the collective appearance of this crew—a sight that would have sent less tolerant boys screaming for the horizon.

Milrose, in fact, preferred these appalling spectres to living students, and confined most of his social activity to the third floor. And he was as happy there as any boy might be in the company of loyal, unpresentable companions.

A day in the life of Milrose Munce was like a day in the life of any ordinary sarcastic youth, if you discount the ghosts and explosives. School began every morning with homeroom, during which the class was told things that Milrose almost never needed to know, generally involving sports.

When homeroom ended with a vicious bell, students were ejected to wallow through a carefully scheduled morning of higher learning. The majority of these students would rather not learn—and the majority, as a consequence, did not. Milrose Munce, however, enjoyed school. He tried not to admit this to anyone but his friends on the third floor, most of whom had also enjoyed school until it cut their lives bitterly short. But among the living, it was not considered admirable to find school anything but a hideous burden.

His fellow students could tell that learning was not much of a burden to Milrose Munce. He did it far too easily, and never looked nearly miserable enough. And his misbehaviour in class—which was prodigious—was clearly a result of having mastered all of the work much too quickly, thus triggering an episode of intolerable boredom.

The lesson being thrust upon the first class today, for instance, concerned the Azores. Now, Milrose might easily have been fascinated by the discussion of a Portuguese community stuck on a sprinkling of tiny, lonesome islands in the very middle of the Atlantic Ocean, except that he had already gone through a short Azores obsession, and knew far more about them than Mr. Colander, the geography teacher. Hence, Milrose was bored out of his brainpan.

Because he was in an especially evil mood, Milrose put up his hand to announce this.

"Yes, Milrose?"

"I'm bored."

It was difficult for Mr. Colander to respond to this. Milrose had made the announcement so politely that it was not easy to identify it as misbehaviour.

"Thank you for your contribution, Milrose."

"You're welcome, sir."

The second period of the day—nominally devoted to Phys. Ed.—was usually a good time to laze about the third floor. After years of dire school rankings in Physics and Chemistry, the school had decided to hold science classes only in the afternoons, after the students had fully woken up. This left the labs open all morning for Milrose to lounge uninterrupted with his friends. Phys. Ed. class, which Milrose rarely attended, lasted an hour and a half, after which his classmates would spend fifteen or so minutes removing their sweaty clothes in the dim grim locker room, showering briefly in the fungus-bearing shower room, then dressing for a dose of poetry in the English room. Today, that gave Milrose plenty of time to assist Deeply Damaged Dave, who was always keen to further his investigations into the complex art of blowing things up.

It must be stressed that Milrose was not evil. He did not have any desire to blow *people* up—not even the people he truly disliked. Nor did he have anything in common with those boys who set buildings on fire, or take assault weapons to school, or torture small animals. He despised these types. He simply had a healthy interest in watching objects fly violently into random pieces.

Deeply Damaged Dave had devoted a great deal of his life—and pretty much all of his death—to the study of this art. Meeting Dave was, for Milrose, a life-altering event. Dave was his mentor. His guru. Deeply Damaged Dave knew the kinds of things that eager young villains like Milrose were desperate to know.

Dave himself was eagerness personified. In fact, if Dave had one flaw, it was this: that his great lust for swank combustibles and glorious catastrophe often resulted in displays somewhat more dazzling than he had in mind. "Why don't we add just a pinch more of this," Dave would say, with scientific glee. "Just to see what happens."

And what happened was always predictably unpredictable.

Today, Dave—not satisfied with what he had learned so dramatically about the properties of rubidium—was keen to investigate the effects of potassium when combined with water. Milrose already had some knowledge of these extraordinary effects. The Chemistry teacher used to be Mr. Juan

Perdido, one of the few teachers with a genuine sense of humour. One gorgeous day he had devoted a lesson to the properties of this nicely dangerous metal.

Now, potassium tends to go bad when combined with air, so it's necessary to keep it at all times immersed in mineral oil. It doesn't like water, however. Like rubidium, potassium—when dunked in water—explodes. During the course of his lesson, Mr. Perdido had pretended to accidentally drop a large chunk of potassium into a beaker of water. He stared at the beaker for a moment with a look of exaggerated terror. "I thought that was mineral oil. Duck!" Upon which the students had hurled themselves beneath their desks. There was a long silence, which Mr. Perdido brought to a close by saying: "Boom." The teacher had enjoyed a good laugh; among the students, however, only Milrose had joined in the merriment. The rest complained to their parents, who arranged to have Mr. Perdido deported.

Milrose had been the only student not to duck, and he was disappointed when deprived of what had promised to be an excellent explosion. Today he hoped to remedy that.

Being the careful, philosophical soul that he was, Dave began by investigating the effects of very tiny amounts of potassium. Quickly, however, this proved tiresome: the potassium would sizzle, but nothing truly *interesting* happened. And so, as he usually did,

Dave caused the experiment to rapidly escalate, until they had fractured a test tube, atomized a small flask, and—for the grand finale—conveyed an impressive beaker to that place into which glassware disappears when it departs this life. Milrose had fully observed this time, but had taken the precaution of doing so from the back of the room. For Dave, being stuck full of shards of beaker was hardly an issue (after all, he had damaged himself in far more serious ways in the past).

"And now," said Deeply Damaged Dave, "we shall fill the entire sink full of water." He turned on the tap, disappeared into the storeroom, and emerged with a giant container of potassium.

"Brilliant," said Milrose.

"This will be true science," said Dave.

"We shall learn from this," said Milrose.

"We shall become wise," said Dave.

Just as he was about to uncap the container in preparation for dumping a massive chunk of potassium into the filled sink, the doorknob rattled. It turned as well, but the door was stuck, so Dave had a moment to spirit the potassium into the storeroom, with great regret.

The door finally popped open, and in peered Mr. Shorten. Mr. Shorten was perpetually furtive, as if he expected an assassin around every corner. Milrose suspected that Mr. Shorten had been a spy

during some war or another, and had in fact survived numerous attempted assassinations. How
then, pondered Milrose, could this man have
become so tedious? If Milrose had been a spy, always
one step ahead of murderous enemies with accents,
he would surely have become even more interesting
than he already was. Of this he was certain.

When Mr. Shorten spied Milrose Munce standing
awkwardly at the rear of the class, the teacher
released a tiny "eep" and instantly retracted his presence from the doorframe. A moment later he was
again peering—perhaps now half convinced that
Milrose was not a trained assassin. He squinted. No,
this was clearly Milrose Munce: obnoxious, ill
behaved, but hardly murderous.

"Munce, what are you doing in the lab? Chemistry isn't for three hours."

"Oh, uh, just . . . doing some extracurricular
experimentation."

"Some what?"

"Adding to my education. Private boy-genius
stuff."

"If you are a genius, Munce, I am a monkey."

"Well put, sir."

Mr. Shorten stopped for a moment in an attempt
to determine whether he had been insulted. He
decided that he had, but then it was necessary to
determine whether Munce had insulted him or

whether he had inadvertently insulted himself. Mr. Shorten could not make up his mind, so he decided to let it pass.

"And your experiment, Munce? What have you been discovering about the mysteries of nature?"

"Well, sir. I filled the sink full of water. As you can see."

"Yes, I can."

"Amazing, isn't it."

"Isn't what?"

"The sink, Sir. Observe how it holds the water."

"Yes?"

"Well, I find it fascinating."

"You find *what* fascinating?"

"How the water remains in the sink, sir. How the sink does not melt, despite being thoroughly soaked. Now, if this were a paper bag, sir, it would accomplish no such thing."

"Munce, if you are a genius, I am an eel."

"Nicely argued, sir."

After this exchange, Milrose Munce excused himself, as he had only moments until English class would begin. He glanced back to see Mr. Shorten gazing thoughtfully at the sink.

Milrose, given that he very much liked to talk, and saw language as a useful weapon of sorts (if not quite as effective as potassium), should have been utterly thrilled by the subject of English. Unfortunately, the subject was taught on the second floor, whose residents had given Milrose an allergy to all things poetic.

Nevertheless, Milrose did enjoy reading literature, as long as it wasn't—strictly speaking—poetry. Shakespeare, for instance, was too much fun to be poetry. This week they were studying *Macbeth*, which featured astonishing amounts of gore and culminated in a fine beheading. A couple of weeks ago it had been *King Lear*; Milrose had been especially impressed by the scene in which Gloucester's eyes were forcibly removed. Yes, Shakespeare was a genius, concluded Milrose Munce (which was not his most original conclusion).

Even more exciting than English was Lunch. Lunch, though not technically a class, was educational.

Milrose considered himself something of a political scientist, and he loved to analyze the class structure of the school. How the Popular ruled over the merely Tolerated, and how these disdained the Unwanted. Over lunch, these differences were easily studied, as the lunchroom was fully segregated: the Popular sat on one side, the Unwanted on the other, and the Tolerated occupied the middle, thus protecting the aristocracy from encounters with the disdained.

Milrose generally sat with the Unwanted, as they tended to be more interesting. This was a mystery to the Popular, who considered Milrose fully capable of being Tolerated, and perhaps even Popular if he made the effort. Milrose, however, considered himself extremely Popular: he was very much liked by the Unwanted. All of this was confusing for everyone but Milrose Munce.

Today, Milrose decided—as an experiment—to talk loudly and happily to Kitty Muell, who was as a result of her shyness pretty much useless in society, and therefore Unwanted. Kitty was a fine girl, and Milrose got a real kick out of talking to her. It was always fascinating to converse with a girl who generally never spoke to anybody, as she was just dying to share all sorts of thoughts and observations.

The Unwanted were expected to speak quietly, as they were presumed to have nothing thrilling to say. Speaking loudly was reserved for the Popular, who almost never had anything thrilling to say but said it with such boisterous conviction that it seemed thrilling, as long as you didn't listen too carefully. And so it was extremely unusual to have someone on the Unwanted side of the room yammering away with gusto. And doubly unusual that Milrose was doing so with a girl who was meekness itself.

It was a superb experiment. The results were almost as interesting as the interaction of potassium and water. The Popular fell into a confused silence, distressed to think that something thrilling was being said on the wrong side of the room. The Tolerated, who of course were dying to be Popular, followed suit. Very soon Milrose was the loudest person in the lunchroom. The Unwanted, heartened by this reversal, began to speak with more confidence. And so began something like a revolution: by the end of the lunch period, great peals of wild conversation consumed the Unwanted side, and completely eclipsed the uncomfortable whispering amongst the Tolerated and the Popular.

If only the rest of the day had been as amusing.

TWO

MILROSE SAW HIS MOOD TURN INCREASINGLY SOUR AS THE DAY WOUND TO A CLOSE. HE HAD BEEN SADDLED WITH A DETENTION AFTER SCHOOL, WHICH MEANT THAT HE WOULD HAVE TO SPEND AN ENTIRE HOUR IN ROOM 117, ON THE FIRST FLOOR. MILROSE AVOIDED THIS FLOOR—A BRIGHTLY LIT PLACE OF SUBTLE HORROR—UNLESS HE WAS FORCED TO BE THERE FOR A CLASS OR DETENTION, AND ON THOSE OCCASIONS HE WOULD VISIT WITH TREPIDATION AND FOREBODING.

He had nightmares about this floor, and they were not easy nightmares.

For the first floor had no ghosts.

The detention was imposed for the normal reasons: Milrose had responded to a teacher's question with a remark that was just a notch too clever. This teacher in particular tended to ask cloddish questions, and was not pleased when a student proved too quick in his response. Even worse was a student like Milrose, who was not simply quick but entertaining, and sometimes obliquely sardonic. The ape-shaped Mr. Borborygmus could never be *sure* that Milrose was being obliquely sardonic, but there always remained that possibility.

"Detention, Munce."

"But why, sir?"

"It should be obvious."

"But it's not!"

"Then you can spend the detention pondering that question. I hope that you figure it out."

This was the closest thing to actual wit that Mr. Borborygmus had ever displayed, and Milrose was impressed.

"I like that, sir. I do. It's sharp."

"Thank you, Munce."

"I mean it, sir! Witty. Pointed. Quick."

"Good."

"You've been studying!"

"Two detentions, Munce."

This afternoon Milrose would be enduring the second of these.

When you are accustomed to being surrounded by your friends—even friends who looked like death warmed over (of course, they had not been warmed over)—it can be very lonely to sit without them. Milrose associated classrooms with comforting thoughts, like violent and messy extinction. He did not enjoy classrooms like this one, where detentions were always held: an airy, sunlit space, with large windows, lovely wooden desks, and no ghouls. Room 117 was an eerie and threatening place.

Milrose was ornery as he made his way down the first-floor hall. He was, however, cheered considerably when he discovered who would be presiding over his punishment. Waiting for Milrose in room 117 was Caroline Corduroy. Ten years before, she had been Cryogenic Kelvin's heartless girlfriend—she was still, to be perfectly honest, quite hot—and she was now a teacher. He was the only student sentenced to a detention today, which meant that he could spend an entire hour subtly irritating Ms. Corduroy, with whom he was a little bit in love.

Ms. Corduroy sat, an almost benevolent tyrant, at the front of the room. Generally, during a detention, Milrose was given a sentence, which he was made to write out five hundred times. The last detention had required: "I will not be sarcastic and superior." And the one before: "I will not be so intelligent in class." Milrose would have to write out these lies five hundred times before he was permitted to go home. This detention, being conducted by the magnificent Caroline Corduroy, was likely to prove a bit less mundane.

"Now let's see. What shall we have Milrose Munce produce, as punishment for whatever appalling thing he has done to deserve this detention?"

"I didn't do anything," mumbled Milrose.

"Of course not. You are innocent. You *look* innocent . . ."

"Do I?" Milrose brightened.

"No."

Milrose darkened.

Ms. Corduroy did not, unfortunately, possess a miniature simian brain like old Borborygmus, and Milrose waited nervously to hear what crushing punishment she was so keen to announce.

"You shall write an epic poem."

"A *what*?"

"Well, a very short epic poem. You shall tell a story in two hundred lines of rhyming couplets."

"Oh please. Give me a break . . ."

"That makes one hundred couplets in all. You may start with: 'Once upon a time / Young Munce was made to rhyme . . .'"

"You can't do this. This is cruel and unusual punishment."

"Unusual, yes. I'm quite pleased with the idea."

"And *cruel*. I'm sorry—there are laws against this sort of thing."

"Not in my classroom, I'm afraid. Get to it."

And so Milrose began to construct what looked vaguely—if you squinted at it and held your nose—like an epic poem. He would occasionally deviate from his task to contemplate the sublime, almost perfect features of Ms. Corduroy. Her nose was a masterpiece of nasal design. Her mouth a magnificent example of that warm organ. And her eyes were, if eyes could be described this way, limpid spheres of boundless ironic detachment. In fact, Ms. Corduroy would be perfect, were it not for a tiny birthmark on her neck, shaped like a killer whale battling a giant squid.

"Milrose, what are you staring at?"

"Oh, sorry, Ms. Corduroy. I was just pondering your birthmark."

"I *beg* your pardon?"

"I mean, I was just wondering who was going to win. The whale or the squid."

"Excuse me?"

"Um," said Milrose Munce.

"Did you just say what I *think* you just said?"

Milrose pondered. "I think I did, Ms. Corduroy. I didn't . . . Well, it's not as if I don't *admire* your birthmark. I mean, I think it's totally great."

"Your opinion of my birthmark is of no consequence."

"Oh. Phew. Well, then, we can just bury the matter."

"That is not what I meant, Milrose. It is the fact that you announced this opinion which is offensive."

"Oh, that's okay. As long as the opinion itself doesn't offend you."

"Milrose, neither the opinion nor its pronunciation is appropriate."

"Did I mispronounce 'birthmark'?"

"You shall serve five more detentions for this!" Ms. Corduroy frowned. She gave it some thought. And with great ingenuity, she immediately figured out how to augment the punishment. "And I will not be presiding over them."

Milrose, mortified and gloomy, resumed his tedious task. Ms. Corduroy, doing her best to assume an expression of utter disdain and offence, occasionally found herself touching the birthmark on her neck. At these moments her face inadvertently softened. Milrose finally noticed this, which lifted his gloom completely.

At last, after great artistic labour, Milrose finished the tiny epic poem; Carolyn Corduroy read it, satisfied, and pronounced it the worst poem ever written by man.

The detention was over, and she stood to leave.

"Um, Ms. Corduroy?"

"Yes, Mr. Munce."

"I'm really sorry about the birthmark remark."

Ms. Corduroy fixed him with an arctic gaze worthy of a rabid Snowy Owl. "Shall we not mention it again?"

"Yes. Good call."

At that moment, there was a knock on the door. Milrose shuddered. It was the kind of ominous knock that, if you have an ear for that sort of thing (and Milrose did), indicates the advent of a dangerous, possibly excruciating, definitely life-altering—in fact, life-threatening—Adventure.

An Adventure, you might think, would wear something more tasteful than a brown polyester suit. An Adventure, although Milrose Munce had never properly formed an image of one in his mind, would surely be less bulbous at the belt, and less bird-chested in the chest. Adventures would not, at any rate, waddle.

This Adventure, however, announced itself in the person of Archibald Loosten, the guidance counsellor.

"I'm sorry to interrupt, Ms. Corduroy . . ."

"That's fine, Archie. Our little detention has concluded."

"Good, good. Milrose, stay right there. We are

going to have a meeting. Ms. Corduroy, you may sit in if you like."

"A *meeting*," said Munce, with mock enthusiasm. "You mean a *session?*"

"No, not a session. An informal dialogue."

Ms. Corduroy, in her capricious mood, decided to stay. She installed herself quietly in a chair at the side of the room, and placed her fingertips together, tent-fashion, in an attitude of amused contemplation.

Mr. Loosten, who affected an insincere, jocular informality with the students, sat partially on a desk, with one foot on the floor and the other swinging.

"Milrose, we have decided that you are in need of Professional Help."

Ms. Corduroy started. This was a more serious matter than she had anticipated. "Perhaps I should leave the room?"

"No, no. Please stay. You might be able to . . . constructively intermediate."

Mr. Loosten enjoyed meaningless phrases, as long as they sounded deeply meaningful.

"Professional Help," said Milrose Munce. "You mean . . . I mean, what *do* you mean?"

"I mean that your . . . behaviour in the sphere of educational interaction is . . . indicative of a requirement for attitudinal reassessment."

"That's the best you can do? Meaningwise?"

"It means, Milrose, that you are not having a normal, well-adjusted relationship with the empty air surrounding you."

"What. I breathe . . ."

"You also converse. You have been noted having conversations. With empty space. With people who are clearly not there."

"Oh. Old family habit . . ." Milrose choked.

"Yes, these . . . behavioural deficiencies are often hereditary. Professional Help is especially useful in such deep, unfortunate cases."

Milrose was incensed. "If you're saying that there's something wrong with my family, then I'm just gonna have to conclude that you're way out of your league, thinkingwise. But feel free to take it up with them. I'm outta here."

The silence that ensued, although Archibald Loosten tried to soften it with a look of bogus compassion, was tense. Milrose, despite his tough words, had not risen to leave.

"Your family is not within our therapeutic purview, Milrose. You are. The law does not permit us to Help *them*. We can, however, Help *you*."

"Yeah, well, thanks. I'll keep it in mind." This time Milrose did rise, intending to make a casual dash for the door.

"Milrose, talking to things that aren't there is not the mark of a well-adjusted young man."

Ms. Corduroy cocked her head. "Have you been having these conversations, Milrose?"

Milrose, without a useful lie at hand, said nothing.

"You have also been noted," said Archibald Loosten, "slapping on the back people who are, again, not there. Which is to say, slapping non-existent backs."

"Just, um, trying to give encouragement to the, uh, air around me . . ." said Milrose, weakly.

"The air does not require encouragement, Milrose. Well-adjusted, normal boys *know* this."

"Oh, I do know. Sure I know. It's just, you know, sometimes I feel the world's not happy enough, so in the occasional moment of, I dunno, satanic inspiration, I just give it a reassuring ol' slap on the back."

"Please," said Mr. Loosten. "Let's not blame this on Satan."

Ms. Corduroy frowned. "Milrose, do you . . . do you *really* slap the air on the back?"

"Course not," said Milrose, sinking further into gloom. "Everyone knows that the air doesn't have a back."

"Then what, Milrose, is it that you are slapping?" said Mr. Loosten, with a sleazy, triumphant smile.

"I dunno. Just swatting flies or something."

"Or something," said Mr. Loosten, as if that explained everything to his great satisfaction. "Or *something*, Milrose. We shall Help you with regard to this 'something.'" Archibald Loosten smoothed the hideous fabric bunched at his fat knee. "Milrose. I am sorry to have to pronounce this . . . but your social engagement with . . . empty space . . . indicates to me—and to others on staff—that you are insufficiently socialized. You have a deficit of real human empathy, which requires you to find companionship in places where companions are manifestly not to be found."

"Which means what in, like, English?"

"I am saying that you, I'm afraid, require Professional Help."

Ms. Corduroy interjected. She knew well how serious this matter was—Professional Help was not invoked except in the most grave situations—and she felt a need to intervene on behalf of poor Milrose, who did not yet know what he was in for. "Archie, couldn't we say . . . Is it not possible to interpret this behaviour as merely quirky? Quirky, yet acceptable?"

"I hear you, Ms. Corduroy. We have considered that. Perhaps Milrose is simply a student who occupies the fringes of normalcy in ways that seem to many truly normal people quite abnormal, but which are not themselves—if irritating—beyond the scale of the acceptably ordinary. This might alter the situation sufficiently that he might not require Professional Help."

"Yes!" said Milrose Munce. "Exactly!"

"The Professionals, however, disagree."

The silence that followed was an even less congenial pause. The severity of the situation was beginning to dawn on Milrose Munce, partially because it was clear that Ms. Corduroy was increasingly distressed.

"A boy who is capable of slapping empty space on the back is a boy who will someday be doing all sorts of very peculiar things to non-existent objects that deserve no such treatment. It is a sign, Ms. Corduroy. We know, statistically, that children who start fires will grow into serial killers and cannibals, and we—or at least the Professionals—have determined that boys who have jocular relations with thin air will grow into, well, abominations."

"Isn't that a bit . . . precipitous, Archie?"

"Yeah, isn't that a bit *extreme*?"

"I am afraid that we must defer to the wisdom of the Professionals in this matter. It is, after all, their Profession."

Neither Milrose Munce nor Ms. Corduroy could conjure a rebuttal, as it was clearly true.

"Now, Milrose. This is hardly the end of the world. It is not a *punishment*. We are doing this for your *benefit*. The point of Professional Help is that it *improves lives*. Your life will, we hope, be *improved*."

"I *like* my life."

"Well, yes. But this is only because you do not realize how miserable you are, deep down. This misery is latent, and hidden, and Professional Help is designed to bring it to the surface."

"You're saying these guys intend to make me miserable!"

"You are already miserable, Milrose. You simply don't know it."

Milrose was in fact becoming miserable, and was fully aware of this. Professional Help? All because he had slapped his good friend Cryogenic Kelvin on the back? All because he liked to chat with a dead friend, whose existence he could not of course reveal to anyone else, or they would think him mad? Milrose had of course considered this: that perhaps he should simply admit that he was interacting with ghosts. But he knew instinctively that this kind of admission would not help his case.

He looked to Ms. Corduroy for support. She could not hide her own growing sadness, and she touched her birthmark, unwittingly, in a gesture of sympathy for poor Milrose Munce.

The first floor was that much more oppressive as Milrose made his way down the hall from room 117. Although he did not fully understand what had been announced during that informal conversation, he was sick with foreboding. Something had changed.

His life, until now amusing, if completely unserious, was turning on some great slow wheel towards something else.

As he dragged himself towards the stairs at the end of the corridor, past terrible classroom doors, he found himself on a collision course with a girl who was moving even more slowly than he was. At first he could only see her hair, as her head was bowed in concentration: clearly her feet, stepping carefully on the floor, were of great interest to her. This hair was unnaturally black, and where it parted in the centre, revealed a complexion unnaturally white.

She was wearing faded crushed velvet, once something like violet: a dress far too long for her, and whose worn fringe trailed behind her like the train of a weird wedding gown. In the front the buttons were undone from the floor to just below the knees, so that her shoes were visible. They were ballet slippers, dyed black. The black ribbons wound about her pale ankles, which were also occasionally visible. She made her way towards Milrose Munce, and he continued towards her, transfixed.

Would she look up in time to avoid their impact? Or would she simply walk straight into him? For Milrose Munce had no intention of altering his course.

It was a game of chicken, but slow and infinitely strange. While it did not precisely lift the heart of Milrose Munce, it did cause him to briefly enjoy his misery: this girl, stepping towards him, seemed the sort of company that misery loves.

She did not stop. Nor did he. Only when they were within a few seconds of a soft collision did she look up, and straight into his eyes, and this look froze them both, midstep.

Milrose smiled. She did not. Nor did she move aside, even now that she was aware of his trajectory. She simply looked blankly into his eyes, as if she could barely see him. Milrose, because he had a tendency to do such things, waved his hand back and forth in front of her eyes to determine whether she were blind. She grabbed his hand with a movement so quick that he shivered: clearly she was neither blind nor catatonic. Her grip was firm as she moved his hand back to his side and placed it there. That's where it belongs.

The eyes were not entirely blank now: they were dimly animated, but by what he could not tell. It did not look like amusement, but it did not look entirely different, either.

"Milrose Munce here."

"I know."

"Oh. Do I know you?"

"I like to think that nobody knows me."

"Well, that's nicely pretentious."

"Thank you."

"So how do you know me?"

"I know everybody's name. I make a point of it. If you know someone's name, you have the upper hand."

"True. You have the upper hand. I have, I guess, the lower hand. So what's your name?"

"If I told you that, I wouldn't have the advantage anymore, would I?"

"True."

"Excuse me." She did not move to the side: it was clear that she fully expected Milrose to accommodate her passage. Which, of course, he did. For she had the upper hand.

As the deliberately nameless girl continued her slow movement down the hall, Milrose tried to collect the last few moments in his mind. Now then. What precisely did she look like? Well, pale. Certainly that was a prominent feature: pallor.

She had what are always termed "delicate" bones, for reasons Milrose had never understood until now. The two bones that appeared above her collar—collar bones?—were so thin and sharp that they did seem as if they required special care. Simply doing up the three buttons at the top of the gown—the ones that were, he recollected, open—would endanger the integrity of those fragile bones. Her face seemed equally vulnerable—structurally, at least—and Milrose was glad they had not in fact collided.

Did her eyes have any colour? No, not that he could discern. They were black, even though he had always been under the impression that black eyes were never truly that shade.

She did have freckles, which did much to mitigate the impression that she was a witch, or—worse— one of those standard-issue girls with pale faces who wear long velvet gowns. Freckles were unexpected. Milrose had the sudden suspicion that she was in fact a flaming redhead, who had subjected her hair to the same treatment that she had her ballet slippers. This pleased him: a redhead, quenched like a fire.

Was she attractive? Always a difficult question. Suffice it to say that Milrose Munce found himself wondering whether she had a birthmark, and what shape it might be.

Something about this peculiar girl put Milrose in mind of the second floor. Even despite such mild irritants as Percy, the second floor did seem the sort of place that the girl in the velvet gown would frequent, were she to enjoy the company of ghosts.

Milrose could not imagine this girl fitting in with his crowd on the third floor. Bored Beulah, with what little flesh she had left, was capable of all manner of subtle gestures, indicating, for the most part, disdain. The girl in the velvet gown was not precisely disdainful. She did seem to have a sense of personal superiority, or at least personal uniqueness, but it was a sincere business, this sense. Milrose could tell that the girl in the velvet gown was in fact sensitive, and perhaps fragile. Beulah, on the other hand, was neither.

No, sensitivity was not Bored Beulah's strong suit. And fragility was hardly a concern—even falling into a vat of hydrochloric acid had left no mental scars. Beulah liked to pass off her truly appalling death with a shrug: "These things happen."

Milrose feared that Bored Beulah, though, would make mincemeat of the girl in the velvet gown. Milrose Munce shivered at the thought of subjecting the new girl, with her frail superiority, to the awesome presence that was the posthumous Beulah. The girl in the velvet gown definitely had more of an air of second-floor-esque pretension.

Before leaving the school that day, Milrose Munce was forced to make a brief visit to the basement. The lockers were all situated in that dripping dungeonous pit, and Milrose always left his homework in his locker before going home.

The feeling of doom was not alleviated by his descent into the basement. Milrose generally found that a vague feeling of personal damnation would accompany this journey into the bowels of the school. (He did like that expression: "the bowels of the school." He had employed it in conversation more than once, to chilling effect.) The basement hallway always reeked of something being unsuccessfully covered up by the smell of something else. Which two smells these were, Milrose chose not to identify.

The lockers were shut, but he knew that those without locks on them were capable of opening at any minute, like the windows of a Christmas advent calendar, to reveal a rotting athletic corpse: Imploded Ig, for instance, who had been practising without a helmet, and while carrying the football had plowed straight into a goalpost (which was itself uncharacteristically unpadded); arrogant Ig whose head was concave, so that only one eye remained spherical, while the other was close to flat—a fried egg with a hazel yolk.

Vain Ig chose to remain locker-bound on this dreadful day. Instead, it was Hurled Harry who threw open the door to a pint-sized locker and howled an ear-splitting greeting.

"Hi, Harry. To what do I owe your dulcet voice?"

"What's 'dulcet'?"

"A word that describes a lot of things, but not your voice."

"You don't look so happy, Munce."

"Yeah, well, we can't all be as cheerful as you. What with our lack of hoofprints and all."

Harry had not been a jock. He had been a jockey. Harry was four foot eleven, which is short for, say, a basketball player, but perfect if you want to sit on a horse. The school did not have an equestrian program—so few have—but Harry had been training at a professional track.

The horses were not fond of Harry, because he was afraid of them. Horses are like that. And so they took every opportunity to drag poor tiny Harry through low-hanging branches, or toss him playfully into pools of manure. He survived the grand majority of these incidents. In fact, he survived all of them but one. Still, that's all it takes, isn't it.

One truly hotheaded horse, Sociopath, was exceptionally contemptuous of timorous riders. Harry had never trained with Sociopath, as the horse's reputation preceded him: six jockeys to date had been maimed by this proud horse, and one of them still required a machine in order to breathe. Harry's mentor, however, a tiny, cruel man by the name of Savonarola, decided that it was time for Harry to overcome his fear, and that Sociopath would be the horse to effect this change. If Harry could tame Sociopath, then he would surely never fear another horse. Note the word *if*.

Sociopath had taken the very first opportunity to toss poor Harry. It is not hard for a horse to toss a boy as diminutive as Harry. And Sociopath had not only the strength to do so but the coordination to aim a human projectile extremely accurately wherever he wished. On this particular day, Sociopath was in an especially criminal mood, and he chose to hurl poor Harry in the path of an entire posse of oncoming steeds. These horses, even if they had wished, would not have been able to slow down before trampling the jockey—and, to be honest, they were too busy competing with each other to give thought to a tiny, useless human in their path.

And so Harry—what was left of him, at any rate—ended up bearing a truly magnificent array of hoofprints, including a prominent U stamped right in the centre of his face.

"So what's bugging you, Munce?"

Hurled Harry was the closest thing to a friend that Milrose had in the basement. It seemed that dead jocks were excruciating in proportion to their size. The larger athletes suffered from swelled heads (this seemed to involve a thickening of the skull, without an actual increase in its capacity), whereas Harry was never permitted to feel physically superior, and so retained an element of humility. Also, the tendency on the part of the basketball players to use Harry as a medicine ball contributed to his modest sense of self. He and Milrose might have been reasonably good friends, in fact, were Harry less annoying.

Unfortunately, Hurled Harry had chosen to compensate for his size through the cultivation of his voice. Harry was loud. Loud, without having anything much to say, and without having the kind of voice you want to hear at all, much less at Harry-like volumes. Even before he had taken to howling and wailing—back when he was alive—Harry's voice had been capable of peeling carrots. Now it could skin whole rabbits.

"What's bugging me? Apart from your screeching? Well, it seems that my world has just imploded."

"Cool. You can bond with Ig!"

"I'd rather bond with a wet fungus."

"That could work."

"So, yeah. Things aren't so hot today. And they're gonna get even less hot tomorrow, I suspect. By the end of the week, they're going to be, like, lukefreezing."

"What's up?"

"Seems they've determined that I need, uh, Professional Help."

"Like a sports doctor?"

"No. More like a brain surgeon. Who works with a fork."

"That does sound unpleasant."

"Actually, I don't know what it means. 'Professional Help.' I just know that I don't want any."

"Can't you turn it down?"

"Apparently not."

"What would happen?"

"Good question. Something very, very bad, I take it."

"Why don't you try?"

"Because I don't want to experience something very, very bad."

Harry thought about this. "Good point." He thought further. "Hm . . . maybe I can help."

"*You're* gonna help? I'm already getting *Professional* Help."

"I mean, maybe I can help you get out of this help thing."

"That would be helpful."

"Dunno what I could do. But I'll think about it. I could maybe enlist some of the guys."

"What, to think with you? The brains on this floor—even when they try really hard—produce things that look more like, I dunno, mushrooms than thoughts."

"What's with you and fungus today?"

"I think it's the basement. The bonny fragrance of mildew. That *is* mildew, isn't it?"

"Nobody's ever identified the smell."

"Charming. Anyway, Harry, I really appreciate your concern. And if you can figure out a way to help, however useless—hey, I wouldn't look a gift horse in the mouth."

"I'll give it the old school try, Munce. Catch you later." And with that he returned to his locker, howled briefly for effect, and shut the door.

The only thing Milrose Munce hated more than a dead jock was a live jock. These too would congregate in the basement, snuffling and grunting like a penned herd of bison.

You would think they would loathe Milrose Munce as much as he loathed them, but—unlike the dead jocks, who were resentful in general—the living jocks had a perverse respect for him. Milrose made such a point of not being athletic that they regarded him as an interesting mystery. Milrose, for instance, would be incensed if he were not chosen last to play on a team. Once he had been chosen second-last for a game of baseball, and he had thrown a dramatic tantrum, breaking a bat in the process. It was all for show, of course—Milrose was not the tantrumic type—but it was a very good show.

None of the living jocks now snapping at each other with wet towels would think to snap one of their wet towels at Milrose, for fear that he'd do something, well, odd.

"Munce! You gonna join us for some rugby?"

"What's rugby?"

"You're joking, right, Munce?"

"Uh, no. When I joke, people melt with laughter. I was asking a question."

"Munce doesn't know what rugby is!"

"What about rugger, Munce? Ever heard of rugger?"

"Somebody who makes rugs?"

"Munce thinks rugger is a guy who makes rugs!"

One of the more helpful jocks was about to go into a long disquisition regarding rugby, its rules and traditions, its fans and foibles, when Milrose sneezed so violently that conversation stopped, for fear he might have broken something inside of his head. This sneeze was a pre-emptive strike: he knew very well what rugby was, and had no desire to learn it again.

"You okay, Munce?"

"Think I broke something inside of my head."

"Oh man. Bubba, call the sports doctor."

"Just kidding. I'm fine. Hey, any of you guys ever needed . . . Professional Help?"

"You mean an outside trainer?"

"No, idiot. He means a physical therapist."

"Actually, forget it . . ."

One linebacker, Sledge, was staring at Milrose with something approaching concentration. "You mean, like, Professional Help?"

"Yeah. Something like that."

"I had some."

Sledge was only human in the loosest sense of the word. He had muscles that would have been far more appropriate in the wilds of Borneo; he had a neck like a squat Ionic column; and he had a very, very low forehead—so low that his hair seemed almost to grow out of his eyeballs. His nose had been broken so many times that it was more like a doorknob, and Milrose wondered whether, by turning that nose, the jock's face might open to reveal the walnut-sized brain behind. He decided not to try: Sledge's other chief feature was a psychotic stare, accompanied fairly often by psychotic behaviour.

"Yeah. They gave me Professional Help. Din't help."

"Er, what precisely did they *do*?"

Sledge's face screwed up in a dull approximation of fear, as if in response to a dull but frightening memory, and he made a low, incoherent noise. He began to move towards Milrose, in the purposeful, automatic way that Milrose associated with homicidal robots, and it seemed best to cut the conversation short.

"Great talking to you, Sledge. As always. Been a pleasure. Gotta go."

THREE

"My son doesn't need Professional Help!"

"Would you prefer he had Unprofessional Help?"

The father of Milrose Munce, whose name was (unfortunately) Mortimer Munce, was stymied by this response. "Well, no."

"There you go. So Professional Help it is."

"What if he requires no help at all?"

"Then he will be helpless."

Mortimer Munce, who was less talented than his son in the art of the quick response, was quite silenced by this argument.

And so the father of Milrose Munce signed the papers, which had been laid out on the kitchen table by Mr. Loosten. Papers that said many inscrutable things, but which amounted to a very simple concept: his son was now in Helping Hands, whose iron grasp it was now beyond both Mortimer and Milrose to loosen. Mr. Loosten confirmed as much.

When Milrose arrived home, some minutes after this momentous signing, he found the guidance counsellor—who had put on a special beige polyester suit for the occasion—half sitting on the kitchen table, with one foot on the floor and the other swinging joyously.

"Mr. Loosten."

"Milrose."

"To what do I owe this modest honour?"

"A simple bureaucratic necessity. All done. Nothing need concern you."

"But I am concerned."

"It's no concern of yours."

"It is as far as I'm concerned."

"Mr. Loosten here has just had me sign some papers."

"What *kind* of papers?"

The guidance counsellor hastily gathered up the documents. He placed them in his briefcase as Milrose repeated his question: "What specific *type* of papers are we talking here?"

"Well, according to Mr. Loosten, it was necessary that I sign a few documents before you could receive the Help which you require."

"Whoa. Dad. You just signed my life away?"

"Well, it wasn't put to me in precisely those terms."

"You just sold me down the river? What were you thinking?"

Mr. Loosten smiled his usual smile of benevolent condescension. "Now, Milrose. Let's not be dramatic."

"Hang on. You mean if Dad *hadn't* signed these papers, I would have been free?"

"Let's not concentrate on the past. It's the future which we're now looking forward to!"

"That's not the *past*. It's ten minutes ago!"

"The past ten minutes. Have passed." Mr. Loosten tucked his briefcase under his arm, in a suspiciously protective manner, and waddled with great speed to the door. "Great to see you, Milrose. Mortimer, thank you for your time."

"Dad, I think you just destroyed my life."

Mr. Munce scratched his head, depressed, wondering whether this were true.

Milrose wandered the house all afternoon in despair. Well, the closest thing to despair that Milrose could muster, which was annoyance. The only way to cure annoyance, Milrose felt, was to annoy somebody else even more. So he decided that it might be a good plan to hang around the kitchen while his mother prepared dinner, and to pepper her with irritating questions.

"Mom, why the deuce did you call me Milrose?"

"Please do not use that word in front of me."

"I'd rather not. But it's my name, and it's your fault."

"I meant the word 'deuce.'"

"Oh. Is it a bad word?"

"I'm not sure. But I suspect it probably was, once."

"Uh, okay. Terribly sorry, et cetera. But why my deuced name?"

"Your father and I decided on Milrose for . . . certain reasons."

"Which are?"

"Reasonable."

She was a maddening woman, his mother, although he loved her, of course: she had perfected a form of stubbornness so subtle that it could barely be perceived. If she did not want to do something, she would simply become slightly absent, and no amount of pressure could make her present.

It was something that only occasionally bothered Milrose, his first name. "Munce" was more of a problem, what with its possible variations: Dunce, Monkey, Muncemeat. And his mother had never had much choice in that one—although perhaps she might have married someone else.

"Milrose," on the other hand, was simply a bit peculiar, and potentially a girl's name. This last problem did not bother him as much as it would have most young males. Milrose was in fact a touch less masculine than many other boys. He had delicate features and longish dark hair, and his intelligent eyes were filled with empathy, warmth, and sarcasm. Rather than sinewy, he could be described as willowy (if you were generous); Milrose had definitely been gifted with brains over brute brawn. He carried these features well, however, and many lunkheaded football captains were truly annoyed to find that some girls found Milrose Munce more attractive than hypertrophic morons.

No, his problem with the name Milrose was more a question of balance. If your last name is Munce—a weird name, at best—then your first name should be something like Jeff, or Douglas. Something solid and uninspired. If your last name is Smith, certainly, by all means pair it with Milrose.

Still, his mother seemed to have had her reasons for this graceless combination, and he wasn't about to elicit them. He rubbed the side of his nose in silence, trying to think of another annoying question.

"So what's for dinner?"

"Food," said his mother. "Followed by dessert."

Milrose stared at her with admiration. His mother was one of the few people on the planet with an even greater gift for sarcasm than his own.

"Isn't dessert a kind of food?"

"Not this dessert. I've decided to poison you."

"Mm. Will it at least taste good?"

"For a minute. And then you will fall into it, face first."

"Are you sure you want to murder your only son?"

"Quite sure, darling. Would you set the table, please?"

As he set the table, Milrose realized that his mother had succeeded in cheering him up. All of those mothers out there who read books by specialists—witless books about how to bring up perfect children—probably never threatened to poison their offspring. His mother, on the other hand, never read these books—and in fact held them in contempt—as a result of which she knew how to make him happy when he was annoyed.

Dinner was indeed food. His mother had baked lasagna, something she did surprisingly well, given that nobody in the family had an ounce of Italian blood and she had never been to Italy.

"The lasagna's great," said Mr. Munce, his mouth still full of lasagna.

"Don't speak with your mouth full, Dad," said Milrose.

"Please don't tell your father what to do," said his mother. "And Mortimer, please don't speak with your mouth full."

They avoided the topic of Help over dinner. It was not an appetizing subject, and neither Milrose nor his father had yet revealed the situation to Mrs. Munce. Both of them, however, thought about it a great deal as they polished off the lasagna.

Milrose was feeling increasingly unnerved—anything that required his father to sign legal papers was probably very serious indeed. Did those papers perhaps relieve the school of responsibility if Milrose were, for instance, horribly maimed in the process of Help? This was the kind of legal paper that Milrose enjoyed, in general, but not when it applied to him. Did the papers perhaps consign him to decades of slavery in the basement of the school? This seemed less likely, but who knew, given that neither he nor his father had read them. Perhaps the papers stipulated that Milrose would have to donate all of his organs to science. Next week.

The vibrant, baroque imagination of Milrose Munce produced numerous variations on this, until he had pretty much exhausted all of the unspeakable possibilities suggested by those papers. At which point dessert was served.

Dessert was not poisonous. His mother had been lying. Dessert was in fact a substance that Milrose valued even more highly than rubidium: lemon meringue pie. He gazed at his mother lovingly. Her intuition was such that she always knew when it was necessary to blindside her son with a massive slice of his favourite stuff.

For some hours after dinner, Milrose wandered about in a joyous lemon meringue haze, but the effects wore off as bedtime approached. By the time he was ready to go to sleep, he was once again obsessing about Help, and dreading the thought of school the next day.

With a heart heavy with annoyance, Milrose set out for school in the morning. The walk was short, especially if you disregarded the signs trying to dissuade you from taking the shortcut along the railway tracks, and as Milrose almost always took this route, he had regular encounters with Severed Sue.

Severed Sue was a not-very-bright young phantom who, when alive, had been wearing headphones while sauntering down the track, and had thought the screeching approach of the train was simply part of the music she was enjoying, until she ceased to enjoy it.

"Hola, Sue," said Milrose to his friend—a friend who came in two very distinct parts, separated by a thin rail's width of air. He tried to disguise his leaden mood.

"Hey, Milrose!" said the half of Sue that contained a mouth.

"What are you up to today?"

"Not much. Thought I'd just watch the trains, you know, go by."

"You do that a lot, I've noticed."

"Yup. Never gets boring."

"Excellent."

It was a general truth that ghosts would not stray too far from one place. Often this was the place where they had died, but sometimes it was a favourite area they had chosen to haunt. Milrose had strained to understand this—"Don't you guys like to *travel?*"—but for whatever reason, most of his friends preferred to stay completely put. This was doubly perplexing to Milrose, given your average ghoul's power of wafting. A ghost could waft great distances with little effort, and if Milrose had been able to do this himself, he would have wafted to the beaches of Mexico during long weekends. Perhaps you really do become lazy when you're dead, thought Milrose.

He rarely gave much thought to his ability to see and converse with ghosts; it was something he had always done, and it seemed quite ordinary to him. From his perspective, however, he was not odd: the rest of the world was weirdly blind.

Once, when he was very young, he had shared with his kindergarten teacher his excitement over making a new dead friend; her response had been so disappointing that he had never tried this again. His teacher had pretended to be excited as well, but Milrose understood immediately that she was merely humouring him. She kept praising his "imagination," and it was obvious, even to a young boy, that he was being accused of making things up. And so he had kept this rare faculty to himself. Or so he had thought. Clearly, he had not been careful enough.

During biology class, despite Kelvin's antics, Milrose Munce could not be cheered. He was as blue as the flesh of Kelvin's forehead. And his chilly friend did his very best: he dipped his finger into Mr. Shorten's coffee between sips, so that the drink went instantly from nicely hot to disgustingly cold. But even the sight of Mr. Shorten spluttering decaf across his desk was not sufficient to lift the spirits of Milrose Munce.

Kelvin enlisted Stuck Stu, who also put on his finest show: he sent off torn bits of himself, one at a time, and a particularly gruesome piece of flesh hung quivering from the tip of Mr. Shorten's nose— but Milrose would not so much as smile.

No, there was no consoling Milrose Munce. A great doom hung upon him, like a wet lab coat.

Milrose had, thus far, assumed that his Help was to be imposed on school grounds, but he had no idea where in that building something as terrible as Professional Help might be inflicted. Surely a special chamber would have to be outfitted? Or a pit lined with soundproofing materials? Milrose had been everywhere in the school, or so he thought, and had never encountered anything remotely like such a place.

Nor did he have any sense of when this process was destined to begin. Would he be given some warning? Or would he suddenly find himself caught in the vise-like grip of a Helping Hand, to be dragged off and improved?

These were the thoughts that consumed Milrose Munce, as he walked with leaden steps down the usually hospitable hall.

It did not help that his next class, Our Natural World, required him to spend an hour on the second floor, among dire dead dilettantes. And the hallway on this floor was unusually pungent today. It smelled, in fact, a bit like a funeral home. A botany experiment had gone wrong in room 212 just after lunch and had introduced a storm of pollen into the environment; the stuff was clustering in corners like yellow dust bunnies, or drifting like tumbleweeds over the sneakers of sneezing students. Milrose assumed that this must be the cause of the overwhelming scent. He was wrong.

At the end of the hall, a young woman with a shock of shockingly red hair was seated in the centre of the floor. As Milrose approached, he noted that she had, pinned on her lapel, a huge white flower of some truly unusual species, and it was this that Milrose Munce had been able to smell half a football field away.

He came closer, and the scent of the flower grew almost overwhelming, in a pleasant if disorienting way.

"Nice flower," said Milrose to the girl, as it was the only thing he could think of to say.

"Thank you," she said. "It's the last member of a dying species."

"Unfortunate."

"It thinks so too. Which is why it's trying so hard. To be a flower."

"Hence the, um, smell."

"Yes. It's trying to be the most florid thing that ever floresced."

"Good for it. And what's your name?"

"I never give out my name. Milrose."

It was, of course, the girl with the long velvet dress, who had indeed been a quenched redhead, and was now returned to full and glorious flame. He decided that he would skip Our Natural World and study this girl instead.

"Ah yes," said Milrose. "Nameless you. I should have realized. It's just that you're wearing something different."

After this clever remark, Milrose chose to investigate what she was in fact wearing. No, it was not a

violet velvet dress. Nothing of the sort. A little bit
velvet, yes, but neither a dress nor violet. She had on
a red plush smoking jacket, a white tuxedo shirt,
black tailored silk trousers with buttoned cuffs, and
the same dyed ballet slippers.

"The slippers, though. Should have tipped me off."

"I'm always prepared."

"For?"

"An audition. You never know when they'll suddenly need a prima ballerina."

"Ah. So you dance."

"No."

The girl stroked the huge florid flower, and in
response it doubled its scent, adding a high note of
almond.

"Cyanide, you know," said Milrose Munce.

"Yes?"

"Cyanide smells like almonds."

"Are you suggesting that my sweet flower might
be trying to poison us?"

"No. Just an observation. Although maybe, as the
last member of a species, it's trying to, you know,
take us down with it."

"Stop being so suspicious. It's just a flower."

"Right. So, um, what are you doing in the middle
of the floor?"

"Visiting."

"Who?"

"Whom."

"Whatever."

"Why?"

"Just wanted to know," said Milrose. "I don't see anyone here."

"They're not here. At the moment. And when they come by, I suspect you won't be able to see them."

Just then, Poisoned Percy floated down the hall, so involved with self that for a moment he did not notice this conversation. Then he stopped. "Munce! Arabella! I did not know you were . . . acquainted."

"Your name's *Arabella*?"

"Excuse me. *Your* name is Milrose."

"Not being critical. Just, well, noting this."

"Noted." Arabella did not look happy. Clearly, it upset her that Milrose now knew her name, thereby depriving her of the upper hand. Also, Milrose sensed, it annoyed her that he was capable of seeing these floating souls.

Milrose, on the other hand, was merely confused. He too was not used to encountering a fellow student with one foot in the grave. While seeing ghosts was something he took for granted, personally, he was comfortable being unique in this way. Milrose decided, however, that if his streak of uniqueness had to be interrupted, he was glad it was this girl who had done so. If it had been, say, the odious harelipped bully, Boorden Grundhunch, he would have been less pleased with the company.

"So we both know Percy."

"In centuries to come, *everyone* will know me. And the name's Parsifal."

"Sure you want that, Poisson, buddy? That's a lot of Christmas cards to send out."

"Poets do not send Christmas cards to their fawning readers."

"Oh. How about to those readers who think you're an excruciating hack?"

"Arabella. I did not think you were of the same . . . temperament as Munce."

"I'm not."

"He does not have a . . . poetic soul."

"Cut me some slack, Percy. You haven't heard my limericks. 'There was a ridiculous ghoul / Who swanned down the halls of the school . . .'"

"That will do, Munce."

"Sometimes I enjoy crass, distasteful company," Arabella explained.

"Wait a moment."

"I was just playing with you, Milrose. I find you refreshing. In a crass, distasteful sort of way."

"That's better."

"So, Munce, to what do we owe the unusual pleasure of your company?"

"Uh . . . well, I like to make a beeline for class

when on this floor—not that I don't love you guys and all, but I'm a bit sensitive, and the sight of poetry makes me weep. So, I was kind of in mid-beeline when I encountered Arabella here. Stopped to chat. Please don't show me any poetry."

Percy chose to let this vulgar comment slide.

"Hey, Arabella—wonder if you know any of my buddies on the third floor. Cryogenic Kelvin? Deeply Damaged Dave?"

"I do not think Arabella would mix well with that company," said Percy with great hauteur.

"Yeah, well, I doubt you'd mix all that well up there either. Come to think of it, they'd probably be inclined to set you on fire."

"I have never been on the third floor," said Arabella. "I have an allergy to most of the elements in the periodic table and have been excused from Chemistry."

"That's a shame. Some of those elements are an awful lot of fun."

"Also, I am quite happy with society here on the second floor."

"What—you hang here a lot?"

"I find it congenial."

"You find this joker *congenial*?"

"Please, Munce."

"Do not be offended by Milrose. I'm sure he is magnificently polite, in general. He is simply depressed," said Arabella. "Milrose has been condemned to receive . . . Professional Help."

Poisoned Percy looked genuinely concerned. "Awfully sorry, Munce. That's terrible."

"Um, Arabella? Is this sort of like everyone's name? You know every lousy thing that's happening to people?"

"No . . ." said Arabella. She stroked her flower. "I too have been designated. As one in need. Of Professional Help."

*f*OU*R*

ARABELLA AND MILROSE SAT TOGETHER ON
THE LAWN IN FRONT OF THE SCHOOL.
MILROSE HAD SUGGESTED THEY GET COFFEE,
BUT ARABELLA HAD INSISTED UPON JUNGER-
BERRIES AND THICK CREAM, WHICH THEY
WERE NOW CONSUMING—SHE WITH DELIGHT
AND HE WITH GREAT SELF-CONSCIOUSNESS.

"You really are ridiculously pretentious," said
Milrose Munce.

"Thank you," said Arabella. "Pass the cream?"

"I didn't know they had wild jungerberries at the
corner store."

"I'll bet you never asked."

"True."

"Imagination, Milrose."

"Imagination is for people with no imagination."

"I shall remember that. Please pass the junger-berries."

"So. Arabella. What did *you* do, to . . ."

"Be considered a candidate? For PH?"

"Yes."

"I didn't precisely *do* anything."

"Then why?"

"I simply *was*."

"Er . . . we all *are*."

"I mean, I was thought to simply *be* the sort of person who needs this kind of thing."

"That's horrible."

"Yes. I'm used to it. My father's in customer service, you see. And my mother's in departmental relations. And I'm . . . well, neither. They've never been able to understand how the two of them, together, could have produced *me*. In fact, they refuse to accept that I am their daughter until it is confirmed through DNA testing."

"That's sick."

"You're kind." She stared off into the distance, where nothing much was worth looking at. "The test results won't be in for a long time. Meanwhile, they've decided that perhaps, with some Help, I might become more like what their daughter was meant to be."

Arabella's until now utterly composed lower lip trembled, a single time. And a single tear, which she refused to acknowledge, made its way from the corner of her eye, down the left side of her nose and around the edge of her mouth, to lodge trembling against her lower lip, which refused to tremble again. Milrose pretended not to notice.

"Yeah, well, who needs them. I hope they get fired for deviant behaviour."

"Thank you." Arabella concentrated fiercely on the jungerberries.

"*My* parents are quite sweet, actually," said Milrose.

"So why have *you* been chosen?"

"Well, it seems that I've been noticed talking to people who do not exist."

Arabella's voice betrayed a hint of uncharacteristic urgency. "They saw you talking to our friends?"

"Well, clearly they assumed I was talking to myself. Or worse: someone *I* saw, who wasn't there."

"But that means that I . . ." Arabella frowned. "Maybe I'm not being sentenced for who I *am*. Maybe they've seen me talking as well."

"That would make sense, wouldn't it."

"It would be nice. Except . . . well, it's not good, is it."

"No. Professional Help strikes me as, in fact, tending towards badness."

"That's not what I mean. I mean it's not good that both of us have been seen conversing with them. I don't know why, but I'm quite sure this is not . . . helpful. To our friends."

"Why? These bozos think we're talking to thin air. They're clearly bent on torturing *us*, not the air we're yacking with."

"Are you sure?"

"Of course I'm sure," said Milrose, who was not sure at all.

"What if . . . I don't know why I'm thinking this, but what if they know about our dead friends? What if they know that we're talking to *them*?"

"And . . . you mean, they don't like it."

"Yes."

"Which would mean that, maybe, they don't like our friends."

Arabella nodded slowly.

They sat in silence, contemplating this vague yet disturbing thought. If this were true, then things were much more complicated, and for some reason considerably more menacing.

"Pass the jungerberries?"

This request, Milrose immediately noticed, was voiced in a voice considerably lower and even more poised than Arabella's. It also emanated from the place over his shoulder, which is not where Arabella sat.

Beside them, having arrived in a way so discreet as to seem almost impossible, lounged an unnervingly well appointed man, whose tie and immaculate suit were especially out of place against the scrawny grass.

Without thinking to pause or question, Milrose passed the jungerberries.

"May I introduce myself?" said the finely tailored man. The question did not seem to permit a response: he was going to introduce himself whether it were desired or not. Which it was not. "My name is Massimo Natica. A pleasure."

It was not.

Massimo—or was it Mr. Natica?—did not partake of the jungerberries he had been passed. He simply held the bowl, cradled in one hand, as he smiled toothfully. Milrose noted that his pupils were unnaturally large, and not precisely circular. He was so closely shaven as to look almost plastic.

"I'm, uh, Milrose."

Arabella did not smile. Her eyes went opaque and inscrutable, as they had when Milrose had first encountered her. "I do not give out my name."

"That's okay, Arabella. I understand."

Arabella was incensed. "You do not know my name. Therefore I forbid you to use it."

"Of course, Arabella. These things are fully understandable."

"With all due respect, Mr. Massimo Natica, I do not think I wish to share our jungerberries with you."

"Understood." And yet he did not pass the berries back to them.

"Who are you? And why are you lounging beside us, uninvited?" inquired Arabella.

"I am Massimo Natica."

"Yes. And?"

"I understand your suspicion."

"Not suspicion. Antipathy."

"Such a perfect day," said Massimo Natica, admiring the weather. "It is a perfect day to commence."

Milrose and Arabella were now silent. This was ominous. They had no desire to commence anything, much less with this slick and vexatious man.

"Do not be concerned. I am not here to hinder you. I am here to Help."

Milrose stood, prepared to run. He felt the urge to sprint, athletically, in a direction away from this Massimo Natica. Since almost every direction pointed that way, he froze, briefly, trying to decide which one. But this brief freeze could not be unfrozen, and he simply stood there.

"Do sit down, Milrose. You and Arabella are enjoying your jungerberries, and you do not wish to interrupt the exquisite perfection of this moment."

"Uh, Natica? You're still holding the jungerberries, so it's kind of hard to enjoy them, isn't it."

"Sit down."

This was not a command; it was not uttered in a

different tone from what Massimo Natica had been employing all along; and yet it somehow caused Milrose to sit down on the grass.

"We shall repose here and luxuriate in this moment, for a moment, and then we shall repair to my office."

"Where you intend to repair us, no doubt," said Arabella, not without a hint of fear in her voice.

"And now that we've enjoyed our introductory moment, I think it is time to remove ourselves from nature and transplant ourselves into the comfort of my little den."

Why did it hardly surprise Milrose Munce that the Den of Professional Help was situated on the first floor? The repugnant first floor, friendless and ghost-bereft?

Massimo Natica led them, somehow—for it was against their will—down the hallway of the first floor.

When they arrived at the library, they turned left.

This would not seem such a momentous act, except that it was impossible to turn left at the library. Milrose had never attempted this, for the simple reason that there was a solid wall to the left, and turning would involve, at the very least, a broken nose.

And yet they turned left. It was amazingly easy to do. The hallway itself turned that way, and all they had to do was follow it. Milrose did not like this at all. He glanced at Arabella, and she too was displeased: the hallway really ought not to go in this direction.

"My little den is a comfortable place. You'll like it very much. We'll spend a great deal of enjoyable time together, in my cozy den. This should make you happy."

The door to this den did not promise as much. It was painted a glossy white, and seemed—simply by its aura—to be heavy and metallic. Set into this ominous door was an unusually small window, which was also unusually high: certainly no ordinary human being was of a height sufficient to put nose to that glass. And set into the glass was a screen of thick wire. The sea-green glass was of a colour to indicate great thickness, as if this glass were made to withstand not simply bullets but shoulder-launched rockets and perhaps even heat-seeking missiles. Milrose sensed, however, that there was not much heat to seek behind this daunting door.

That this was the door to the den was indicated by Massimo Natica's proud stance before it. He turned to Milrose and Arabella, and his expression was one of profound appreciation; an expression that beckoned them to join in his exaltation of this lovely door.

They did not.

He produced from his pocket a gruesome modern key—the sort that would drive any would-be burglar to despair—and fitted it into what must have been, internally, a gruesome modern lock. The sound this lock made as it opened was itself complex: a series of clicks and whirs, punctuated by what seemed— could this be?—the cry of distressed rodents.

The light that shone from the opened door did not. Which is to say, there was certainly light behind the door, but it did not shine. The light simply sat there, heavily, like the smell in the basement. Massimo Natica stepped graciously aside and issued his two wards into the den beyond.

The words *comfortable* and *cozy* seemed to vie with each other for status as the bigger whopping lie with respect to Massimo Natica's den. Even the word *den* was a ridiculous misnomer, if meant in the sense of a place you might put your feet up to read a good book. On the other hand, thought Milrose, aren't dens also where innocent people get thrown to the lions?

Displayed in various places around the den were singular objects, some propped against walls, others in glass vitrines—possessions that were clearly dear to the den's proprietor. The cattle prod was perhaps the most unnerving, even though it was clearly an antique, with prominent wiring and an old-fashioned battery. The pitchfork too was old-fashioned, although it looked as if it could still do a good job in those areas where pitchforks come in useful. The prod occupied its own special glass case, but the pitchfork was propped lazily against the wall. The most elaborate display was a line of framed strait-jackets, stretching all the way across the wall: they had been arranged in historical order, to illustrate the evolution of that garment over time.

And in the centre of the room was a group of plump chairs and a sofa.

Massimo indicated these, expansively. "Why don't you make yourselves comfortable."

There were numerous equally appropriate responses to that question.

"I can see that my antiques have you a little appre-hensive. Understand that I collect these objects simply to remind us of how far we have come in the Help-giving process. How much more civilized we are!" He nodded in satisfaction, evidently agreeing with himself. "Well now. Time to sit down and get to work. Try this comfy chair."

Massimo patted one of the comfy leather chairs, and indicated to Arabella that it was hers. He then patted the comfy leather sofa, and indicated to Milrose that this was his.

Arabella sat on the chair, rigidly, as if it were a bed of nails. Milrose, on the other hand, expressed his contempt by stretching out on the sofa, with his feet up on the armrest.

"There we are," said Massimo Natica. "All comfy."

If he uses that word one more time, thought Milrose, I will fetch the cattle prod.

"Now then. Time to get fully acquainted. We're going to be good, good friends. And we're going to get to know each other very well. What we are about to engage in is called Intensive Help. It is by far the best kind. You will be Helped during the day, and while you sleep here, you will be Helped during your dreams."

"Hang on!" said Milrose Munce. "We have to *sleep* here?"

The sleeping quarters were approximately as winning as the den itself. A low doorway led off one wall of the huge room—so low as to require even Arabella, who was not all that statuesque, to bow her head. Milrose insisted that they have a good look at this bedroom before they commenced with any further Help, and Massimo Natica—with a smiling hint of impatience—agreed.

The room was without windows. Come to think of it, Milrose came to think, the entire den was windowless, with the exception of the fortified glass set into the entry door. The bedroom was, however, unusually tall, perhaps three or four stories. The ceiling could barely be seen in the gloom. For the moment the only light was what poured in (slowly, like molasses) through the open door.

Apparently, Arabella and Milrose were to sleep in a bunk bed. It was not an ordinary bunk bed. It had mattresses, one on top of the other, connected by a ladder, but it had about twenty of these, arrayed in a tower.

"Feel free to choose!" said Massimo Natica. "I shall in fact come to some conclusions, based upon which bed you each decide to occupy."

Milrose thought it might be nice to sleep at the top of a tower of beds. On the other hand, rolling out of bed by mistake would be a dramatic and serious affair. Sleeping had never struck him as an adventurous activity, but then much of what he was now experiencing was new.

"I shall take the third bunk," said Arabella.

"Ah," said Massimo Natica. "For any particular reason?"

"Yes," said Arabella.

Milrose pondered his choice.

"I shall wait until you are far from this room before making my decision," said Milrose. "Feel free to come to a conclusion based on that."

After this small and depressing episode, the two found themselves once again occupying their respective chair and sofa, in preparation for whatever might be inflicted upon them. Massimo Natica had a glowing smile upon his absurdly shaven face, as if he had already accomplished great things in the way of Helping his two patients.

Is that what we are? wondered Milrose Munce. Patients? He lay on his sofa, doing his best to reduce the voice of this man to an undifferentiated drone in his ears. Milrose was pretty good at not listening. He had practised this rigorously in the classes of Mr. Borborygmus, so that he could sit through an entire lesson without having to take in any of that teacher's useless information.

As Milrose was in the process of not listening, he examined the ceiling above him. It was certainly not an exceptional ceiling—with one exception. It had a door. Now, the occasional ceiling does have a door—a trap door, which leads in general to an attic. This, however, was not a trap door. It was a door door. It had a doorknob. It opened out, apparently, into mid-air. In that sense it was a dangerous sort of door: Milrose could imagine someone on the other side opening it and falling, bellywards, onto the floor. Then again, it was unlikely that anyone opening that door would be unaware of the fact that they were horizontal while doing so.

Massimo Natica droned on, and Milrose spent the entire drone daydreaming, but Arabella was taking a morbid interest in what the man was saying.

Later, when they were lying in their respective beds, Arabella explained to Milrose what it was that Massimo Natica had said.

"It seems," said Arabella, "that we are to be fully erased."

She had to say this very loudly, as Milrose had decided that he did indeed wish to sleep on the topmost bunk.

"We are to be rubbed out, like a bad essay written in pencil. And then I guess we get recomposed, like a better essay written in ink."

This was not the kind of thing that Milrose wanted to hear, but it was not unexpected.

"He went into a very long explanation, trying to justify this. I was not convinced. Are you convinced, Milrose?"

"What do you think?"

"I thought so."

"Think again."

She thought again. "Yes, I think I know your thoughts."

"Who do you think he is?" said Milrose.

"I don't know. I haven't yet figured out *what* he is."

"Well, a Professional, clearly."

"Did you see a diploma on his wall?"

"No."

"Professionals almost always have diplomas on their wall. It's a point of pride."

"Right. I say we search for the diploma tomorrow. If he doesn't have one, then he's a fraud."

"Wouldn't it be nice if he were a fraud?"

"Yeah. I'd like that. We could torture him with that little fact. Until he broke down and ceased to Help us."

They paused to enjoy this possibility.

"You know," said Milrose, "there's a door in the ceiling."

"Really?"

"Yup. An ordinary door. Except it opens downwards. Or perhaps upwards."

"Into the second floor?" asked Arabella.

Milrose considered this, with growing excitement. "Yes! That's exactly where it would open into. Or out of. Man, I never thought I'd welcome the thought of seeing Poisoned Percy, but it would be great to have him here."

"He's not so bad, Percival."

"He's a pompous, self-obsessed, mediocre bore."

"I do believe you are jealous, Milrose Munce."

Milrose snorted. And then he realized that he was indeed jealous. He was not sure why. It shouldn't really bother him, should it, that this ghost was friends with Arabella? He changed the topic. "It's funny, isn't it, that there are no ghosts on the first floor. Ever thought about that?"

"There are rumours," said Arabella.

"Oh yes?"

"Yes. On the second floor, they talk about this a lot. It's not certain what happened, but there are very distinct rumours."

"Do tell."

"Well, it's a bit weird. And disconcerting."

"Yeah, well, that seems to be a theme today."

"What Percival says"—and once again, Milrose felt that utterly inappropriate twang of jealousy—"is that there was an exorcism."

"Wow."

"Yes. It was once a favourite haunt. So the story goes. But the staff banded together and petitioned the mayor to put up funds for a good exorcist, who came and cleaned it out."

"This gives me the creeps."

"They're not too happy about it on the second floor, either. I mean, it's nothing more than super-stition these days, but nobody dead dares set foot on the first floor, for fear of . . . well, nobody knows what they're in fear of. But it's definitely very frightening."

Milrose did not feel like thinking about this at the moment. And so, as generally happened by default when he did not wish to think, he thought about food. "What do you think we get for breakfast?"

"I don't know. Cold porridge and stale bread? That's the tradition, isn't it."

Dinner, in fact, had not been that bad. Massimo Natica had left the room briefly, counselling them to avoid touching the cattle prod, and had returned with a tray laden with food. Not great food, but passable.

He had also brought ridiculous pyjamas—three sets each—so that they might have something ridiculous to wear. I suppose this indicates, Milrose had thought grimly, that we'll be here for at least three days.

During the silence following the contemplation of tomorrow's breakfast, Milrose noted that Arabella had begun to climb the ladder towards his most elevated bed. His heart, which seemed to be doing unexpected things, did a triple back flip with a half gainer.

He wondered whether she had a birthmark, where it might be, and what it might look like. He could very much imagine her having, for instance, a birthmark on the sole of her foot in the shape of a sneezing gondolier. This wonderment would plague him increasingly, despite his allegiance to Ms. Corduroy's birthmark. Clearly, thought Milrose, I am capable of pondering two birthmarks at once. I suppose that makes me unfaithful, mentally. And perhaps shallow. But that was okay, as Milrose Munce did not mind being shallow.

Arabella's ascent, however, was purely practical. She wished to be much closer to Milrose so that they could converse quietly. It was not clear that Massimo Natica was listening in on their conversation, but neither was it clear that he was not.

Arabella, who was mildly afraid of heights, was happy when her brief climb was complete, and she was lying, heart athump, in the second-highest bed.

"There is a spring in this mattress," said Arabella, "which is very slightly less stiff than the other springs. It causes a tiny depression. Which depresses me."

"You are ridiculous," said Milrose fondly.

"I wonder," plotted Arabella, "whether, when Massimo Natica goes out to fetch our next meal, we might ambush him in some exciting way when he returns."

"I was thinking much the same thing. What I wouldn't give for a nice chunk of potassium just now."

"That is an element in the periodic table?"

"Yes. A personal favourite. Combined with water, it would do excellent things to this Massimo Natica. Rubidium's even better stuff, but it's been banned from the lab ever since Dave . . ." Milrose caught himself. He considered Arabella's delicate sensibilities. "Uh, never mind."

Milrose Munce furrowed his brow, which set his brain in motion. What would Ms. Corduroy have come up with in this situation? She who was so adept at conjuring malevolent punishment? Certainly she would be smiling, with her patented evil smile, and agreeably evil thoughts would be drifting into her happy mind. Milrose smiled a devilish smile, hoping that this might aid him in emulating Ms. Corduroy's thought processes. It did. "Got it," he announced.

"Yes?" said Arabella, with the closest thing to excitement that she ever permitted herself.

"We'll stand on either side of the door. You'll hold the cattle prod, and I'll hold a straitjacket. When he enters, you know, bearing our cold gruel, you'll zap him with the cattle prod; and while he's twisting up in pain, I'll put him in the straitjacket. Then we'll prop him up against the wall, where the jacket is supposed to be hung, so as not to interrupt his precious historical display."

"Yes," said Arabella, with the same approximation of excitement. "And I shall curtsy politely."

"Yes!" said Milrose Munce, who was always happy to express full and delighted excitement. "And I shall say something sarcastic."

"That will be a nice touch," Arabella agreed.

ʄIVE

MASSIMO NATICA, UNSPEAKABLY WELL SHAVEN, OPENED THE DOOR AND ANNOUNCED THAT BREAKFAST WAS READY.

This was a terrible disappointment. It meant that he had already left to fetch the meal, and was now fully returned, which would give them no opportunity to prepare their ambush. The battle would have to wait until lunchtime.

"Something we have not yet addressed, and which clearly must be addressed over the course of our Professional engagement, is the matter of voices."

"What, you don't like the way we talk?"

"I mean the voices which you both apparently hear, even when nobody is speaking."

Milrose caught Arabella's worried eye.

"It has been reported to me by the staff of your

exalted school that you have both, on numerous occasions, been found discussing matters with the unpopulated air in front of you. Long one-sided conversations have been witnessed. And you, Milrose, have been seen laughing at jokes whose punchlines were not delivered."

"Can't be helped, Massimo babe. Family trait. My great-grandmother used to deliver long nagging tirades at her needlepoint. And she would conspire with her brooches."

"Part of our process here is to cure you of your debilitating family traits."

"Sure, man. Cure away. I hate it when the compost sings to me. Highly distracting. Terrible voice, too. And really lousy taste in music."

"Tell me, Mr. Natica," said Arabella with cool calculation. "Do *you* ever find yourself hearing voices from places where voices ought not to issue?"

"Absolutely not! Which is why I confer Professional Help, rather than receiving it."

"Never heard even a little peep of unexpected chatter, guy?" asked Milrose.

"I assure you, that is not in my nature. And were it, I should have to immediately resign my position and join you in this most effective therapy." Massimo Natica laughed heartily at the absurdity of this scenario.

"How do you propose that we silence these

voices, Mr. Natica?" asked Arabella, with her very best insincerity.

"Ah. Well, that will tax my Professional powers to their fullest. But it can be done."

"Speaking of your Professional powers, dude— where's your diploma?"

A pause followed this question. Was this a potential opening, an avenue of assault, a chink in the superlative suit? Could he possibly be without diploma?

"I have always considered Professionals who prominently display their diplomas to be unProfessional."

"I can certainly understand that," said Arabella. "And your admirable lack of vanity makes it impossible for you to descend to the level of those narcissists. Who did you say your tailor was?"

"Natica, buddy. I have no problem with your keeping your diploma in a drawer. As long as there is, you know, a drawer."

"I cannot understand why my furniture would concern you in the slightest. Now then. Let us discuss the tactics we shall employ to rid your unfortunate heads of these intrusive and unwelcome voices."

"Cattle prod?" asked Milrose.

"Certainly not. Although we *have* found cattle prods effective in this regard."

"Pitchfork?"

"I'm afraid the pitchfork has never proved much use in the silencing of voices."

"Surely it would be hard to hear voices with a pitchfork stuck deeply in the brain?"

Massimo Natica smiled. The precise content of that smile—apart from the teeth—was difficult to discern. Milrose Munce wondered whether this little parodic suggestion might have been a tactical error. Best not to give ideas to this possibly fraudulent Professional.

"Perhaps, Milrose, perhaps. But that would fall into the category of antique therapies, and I like to employ only the latest techniques. Now, what we shall do is this. Arabella, I would like you to stand behind Milrose. Very good. Now, I would like you to say something."

"Diploma," said Arabella.

"Uh, yes. Very good. Did you hear that, Milrose?"

"Hard not to. Given that I have ears and all."

"Good. This is going marvellously."

"Gosh, this is modern," said Milrose.

"Thank you," said Massimo Natica. "Now. Arabella. I would like you to simply mouth a word, without making any noise."

"Fraud," mouthed Arabella, without making any noise.

"Good," said Massimo Natica, who of course had not heard the mouthed word. "Milrose. What did you hear?"

"Is this a trick question?"

"A simple question. What precisely did Arabella just say?"

"Er, 'unprofessional'?"

"Is that what you said, Arabella?"

"No. I said 'fraud.'"

Massimo Natica's smile was stuck, it seemed, like a scratched record.

"Lovely. Yes. Good. Now, I would like you to say a few words, out loud, but in between those words I would like you to occasionally insert a mouthed word."

"This is great fun," said Milrose, yawning.

"You are a fraud," said Arabella. Between the words *a* and *fraud* she mouthed the word *consummate*.

"Now what did you hear, Milrose?"

"You are a fraud," announced Milrose, with great pleasure.

"Superb!" said Massimo Natica, through clenched teeth. "You are not having trouble with voices at all today. Not at all. You are hearing what is said, and not hearing what is not said."

"To get to the other side?" said Milrose.

"I beg your pardon."

"That's the answer, isn't it?"

"The answer to what?"

"The question you just asked. 'Why did the chicken cross the road?'"

"I didn't ask any question," said Massimo Natica with concern.

"Oh no," said Milrose, with false alarm. "I must be hearing voices. Even worse: voices telling bad jokes."

"I feared as much."

"Darn," said Milrose. "Cattle prod."

"I think we should save that as a last resort," said Massimo Natica. Milrose again immediately regretted this comment. "Well, then. Professional Help it is. I have a whole plethora of techniques."

"I hope we don't have to go through the entire plethora," said Arabella.

"Yeah, me neither. 'Cause at the end of the plethora lurks the cattle prod."

"Okay now. Milrose, I want you to cover one ear with your hand. If you hear a voice, let me know which ear it enters."

"Will do. Do you also want to know which ear it exits?"

"That is unimportant."

"Okay, your voice just came in through the covered ear."

This perplexed Massimo Natica, so much that he reached for the next technique in his plethora.

"Okay now. Arabella, I want you to put your left ear up against Milrose's right."

It is hard to express how greatly Milrose enjoyed this new technique. He did his best to play along, hearing voices in the correct ear, so that he would not have to remove his cheek from Arabella's warm counterpart.

"When I put my ear to yours, Milrose, I can hear the sea."

"Thank you, Arabella. I am hollow, it's true."

"It's a nice noise. Soothing."

"Does it *say* anything?" asked Massimo Natica with excitement.

"It says 'whoosh,'" said Arabella.

"Which what?"

"Not 'which.' 'Whoosh.'"

"What language is that?"

"One of the oceanic languages, I imagine."

"Fascinating. Okay now. Together, I want you to repeat after me: 'Down, voice! Away!'"

"Down, voice," said Arabella, with an astonishing lack of enthusiasm. "Away."

"Down, voice!" said Milrose. "Down, boy! That's a good voice. Here's a cookie for you."

"And what do you hear now?"

"I hear a voice scampering off into the distance," said Arabella.

"Wonderful! We are making tremendous progress!"

"Good," said Milrose, cheek to cheek. "I can feel that this is by far the most effective technique. A couple of weeks of this, and I'll be cured of those unsightly voices for sure."

"My cheek is getting warm," said Arabella.

Milrose blushed. He knew that her cheek was getting warm because he was flushing. What is the difference, pondered Milrose, between blushing and flushing? I suppose you never blush a toilet . . .

"Those voices are getting fainter!" said Milrose. "I can hear it! This is a stunning technique. You are indeed a Pro, Massimo. Right up there with the best of them. After a few months of this, I'm going to be a new man."

"Good!" said Massimo.

"Yup. After a few years of this, I'm going to be about as cured as they get. Smoked meat."

"Milrose, if we spend entire years cheek to cheek, I suspect we shall melt into each other."

"Yeah. Romantic, huh?"

"I was thinking of it more as a medical issue."

The technique was beginning to render Milrose delirious. He was close to being able to hear all sorts of generally absent noises: the waltz of the spheres, for instance. You can cure me all you want, thought Milrose. As long as I'm not cured.

The morning was passed thus conjoined, and Milrose spent much of that time wondering whether Arabella was enjoying the experience as much as he was. She, of course, remained madly inscrutable, as always.

At last lunch was announced. "Well now," said Massimo. "That concludes our first morning of Help.

Patients are often excited to discover how helpful Help is, even this early on in the process. You are probably very excited."

"How many 'patients' have there been, as a matter of interest?" asked Arabella, with a voice that expressed the very opposite of excitement.

"Oh, lots. You are very lucky to have my undivided attention. Why, sometimes every single bed is filled with a student requiring Professional Help, and I suspect, sadly, that some of them do not receive the individual care that they deserve."

"How tragically unfortunate for them," said Milrose.

"One moment," said Massimo Natica. "One moment and we shall lunch together."

Milrose and Arabella glanced at each other, suddenly nervous and giddy. How much time would they have in which to prepare their ambush? Milrose had spent much of the morning trying to figure out a way to include the pitchfork in the mix.

Mr. Natica sauntered casually to the door, and he inserted his repulsively modern key in the lock. When he turned the key, the whirs and clicks ensued, this time accompanied by the sound of a small mammal being mercilessly teased. He opened the door. Arabella and Milrose unconsciously assumed the stance of sprinters about to plunge into a race.

But Massimo Natica did not leave the room. He opened the door, and was passed a tray of food by someone that neither Arabella nor Milrose could see. Milrose did glimpse the hands and forearms of the person delivering the tray, however, and it did not hearten him. The hands were huge and barely human—they might have looked appropriate attached to the end of Sledge's thick arms. And the white medical shirt the man was wearing seemed about four inches too short, which suggested that his arms were about four inches too long.

Despair occurred to Milrose Munce.

Lunch was, like dinner and breakfast, not too bad. The sandwiches were fresh. Milrose sniffed them for the characteristic almond smell of cyanide, but he could detect nothing.

They lunched in silence. Neither Milrose nor Arabella smiled, although Massimo Natica smiled enough for all three of them. He managed to smile while eating, which was an astonishing feat, and not admirable.

Was yesterday's dinner the very last chance they would have to subdue and conquer their host? Milrose Munce wanted to kick himself. Even now Massimo Natica might be hogtied on the couch, and they might be happily dancing in the sunshine, dining on jungerberries and cream, and delicately approaching the topic of Arabella's birthmark.

Arabella glanced at the door in the ceiling and pondered whether some special combination of words might cause it to swing on its hinges. "Open sesame," perhaps? No, that did not seem probable. This was not the sort of room where exotic commands were likely to have any effect. Perhaps she could just say, "knock knock." And somebody behind the door would answer, "who's there?" But this would require a punchline, and Arabella could not think of one.

Arabella's flower was having an increasingly difficult time in this den. It wheezed asthmatically during lunch, and occasionally coughed. Arabella stroked it with concern.

Massimo looked with suspicion at Arabella's flower. "Do you think that your flower is a *normal* flower?"

"You leave my flower out of it."

Massimo smiled even more broadly, to reveal a distressing number of superb teeth. "Now, Arabella. It was an innocent question. We are not concerned about your flower."

"Well, *I* am concerned about my flower."

Massimo narrowed his eyes, cleverly. "And do you think that's *normal*?"

Arabella narrowed her eyes, murderously. Massimo did not seem to notice.

"This is what I want you to consider as we progress through Help. I want you to think about what you are doing, and whether it is what you would expect of a normal, well-adjusted young person."

That afternoon, and over the next days, they laboured to give their Helper the false impression that they were being Helped. The therapy consisted mostly of silly exercises aimed at silencing voices and enhancing normalcy.

The exercises were so excruciatingly moronic that Milrose would have refused to engage in them on principle, but—for reasons neither he nor Arabella could determine—disobedience was simply not an option. It was a talent the Professional Helper had: when he was set on them doing a certain thing, they had no choice but to meekly obey. Perhaps he was a magician? Had he put something in their food? Milrose wondered.

They made no progress in their plans to overcome Massimo Natica, to punish him and escape. Far from it. Every day reinforced the difficulty of the task: while Natica might have lacked concentration when it came to noting their relentless efforts to insult him, he was clearly aware of their conspiracy, and left them no room whatsoever to manoeuvre.

Every night they sat on the top bunk and embellished their plans for revenge and escape, and nothing the least bit practical emerged.

"I wonder if we shall grow old here," wondered Arabella. "Perhaps that is how we shall escape. We'll be here for so many years that Massimo Natica will grow ancient and die, and then we can take our chairs and wheel out into the sunshine."

"Now that's a joyful thought," said Milrose.

"Well, it's the only plan I can come up with this evening."

"We're getting pathetic. Come on—where's our famed ingenuity?"

Both of them knew that they were not yet widely famous for their ingenuity. But surely they would be, were they to figure out a way to extricate themselves from this Helpful situation.

"Milrose, one thing I've been pondering: Massimo Natica seems keen on preventing us from hearing voices, but he doesn't seem to have any idea where those voices come from. Don't you think it's odd that he is, apparently, completely unaware of ghosts? I mean, if that's his *job*—to make students stop seeing them—surely you'd think he would *know* about them."

"Not knowing about anything hasn't stood in his way thus far."

"True."

"He's probably like a professional hit man. You know, you just hire him to go off and whack a bunch of guys, but you don't tell him *why* he's doing it."

"I'm not thrilled with that analogy, Milrose."

Nor was Milrose himself. This terrible possibility had in fact occurred to both of them. How else would you prevent students from seeing ghosts? Or, more to the point, from *talking* about what they could see? Perhaps Massimo Natica was truly a Professional, but not the kind of Professional that he advertised. In fact, Milrose noted to himself, hit men in movies were often immaculately dressed.

"Well, let's hope we manage to escape before we get whacked."

"I must confess, I'm not fond of that expression, Milrose."

"Okay, then. 'Cured.' I hope we get out of here before we get good and cured for good."

"That's a sensible hope," said Arabella.

"Anyway, remember: what we've been told is that we're being Helped because we hear non-existent voices. There's still no reason to assume that anyone knows we're hearing actual voices, much less ghosts. So, no reason, really, to do us in. And even that would be no reason to do us in. Would it?"

He considered putting his arm around Arabella to comfort her, but he had an attack of cowardice, which caused his arm to freeze and cleave to his ribs. So instead he changed the topic. "You know, I've been thinking. What's everybody on the outside doing while we're locked in here? I mean, your parents are probably pretty happy . . ."

This was also clearly not the right thing to say. As she stared up at the ceiling, Arabella had produced a single tear, which emerged from the corner of her eye, wended its way down the side of her face and lodged uncomfortably in her ear.

"I'm sorry, Arabella. That was insensitive. It's an old family trait, insensitivity . . ." But this did not seem the right time for an "old family trait" joke, so Milrose did not complete the remark. "Anyway, you'd think that my parents would be, I don't know, at least complaining to the Parent-Teacher Association. I mean, yeah, Dad signed the documents and whatever, but there has to be *something* they can do."

"It is a terrible thought," sniffed Arabella, "that nobody is thinking of us at all."

And at that moment, a very faint and pretentious voice filtered through the ceiling above.

"Arabella? Is that Arabella?"

"Milrose, actually."

"Oh, Munce," said the voice, with palpable disappointment. "Are you wearing Arabella's flower? I am inhaling the distinct scent of almonds."

"Percival!" said Arabella, with what approached excitement, but remained of course a few feet away.

"Ah. Arabella. I so hoped it was you. Although the presence of Munce diminishes the experience somewhat. Are you all right?"

"In a manner of speaking. It's been a pretty disquieting time."

"We have been worried. They're not . . . harming you, are they?"

"Well, they're certainly doing damage to my blithe equanimity. Can you help us get out of here?"

"I am not sure. We shall certainly try. As you know, we have . . . trouble with the first floor. It may not even be possible to descend. Nobody knows, really."

"But maybe we can climb up."

"Stunning idea, Arabella! You have always evinced superior imagination."

"Um, like, when all this blather is complete," Milrose said, "can we maybe concentrate on *how* we're going to accomplish this floor-hopping?"

Percy sniffed. "One man's blather is another man's poetry."

"Exactly."

"There is a door," said Arabella. "It's not the kind of door that we generally use. We the living."

"A door! That's certainly a hopeful sign."

"Yes, but it's the kind of door that would probably be more useful for you. To . . . descend."

The silence that followed spoke of cowardice.

"Well then. Any other ideas?"

"Come on, Percy. I thought you poets were all about experiencing extreme emotions. Like rank terror."

"Munce, you will never understand the way of the artist."

"Percival," said Arabella, "where precisely *are* you?"

"That is a fine question. I don't really know. I inhaled the scent of almonds, as I say, and somehow found myself turning left where I've never been able to turn left before."

"Yeah, that's kind of where we're at. To the left of possibility."

"Do you think we'll all have trouble returning?" mused Arabella.

This unwelcome thought had almost occurred to Milrose Munce a number of times, but he had always shoved it back into his unconscious, where it was less intrusive.

"Let us pierce that wall when we come to it," said Poisoned Percy, pleased with his metaphor.

"Piercing *floors* is what we should be thinking about now, poetry boy. Any bright ideas?"

"I'll have to give this some thought."

"Well then, we don't have much hope, do we."

"Please curb your ironic tendencies, Munce."

"Percival," said Arabella, "perhaps it's best if you return to consult with the rest of the dear departed. I imagine a plan will emerge."

"You always did have the most magnificent imagination, Arabella."

"Stow it, Percy. If I throw up, I'm going to be annoyed. Now, something you might do, if you're in the mood to be useful, is contact people more useful than yourself. The guys we want here are my friends on the third floor."

"I do not have . . . social contact with that floor," said Percy with disdain.

"Yeah, well, have no fear: I doubt they're gonna want to socialize with you either. A quick message will do. Something along the lines of, 'Milrose and Arabella are in trouble; I'm a useless poet; can you guys help?'"

"Poetry is not supposed to be useful."

"Right. In particular, I want you to get in touch with Deeply Damaged Dave. He's an expert at . . . well, things. And Kelvin. Talk to Kelvin. He can maybe lead the assault."

"Do you mind, Percival?" asked Arabella.

"If you think it would help, I shall have . . . a brief word with these 'people.'" Percy sighed. "And now, I shall attempt to make the arduous journey back to my compatriots."

"Alternately, you could just, like, walk there. And lie about it later in a rancid poem."

"I shall imagine that I did not hear that, Munce."

"You always did have the most splendiferous imagination."

SIX

MILROSE MUNCE AND ARABELLA SAT
TOGETHER ON THE TOPMOST MATTRESS AND
SPOKE NERVOUSLY.

"Do you think he'll make it back?" said Arabella, implying, amongst other things, that it mattered to her whether something happened to Poisoned Percy. Milrose heard this implication with a sense of evil hope combined with tortured acknowledgement that Arabella actually cared whether this ponce were to meet some punishing fate.

"That would be a good sign. Sort of. Except that ghosts find it a lot easier to go through, you know, walls. If he can make it back, it doesn't mean that we can."

"Still, it is very exciting that we have been contacted," said Arabella, with cool detachment.

"It would be more exciting if it had been anyone else. I hope that silly ghoul does contact my friends on the third floor."

"I do think you are displaying a very uncharacteristic sign of jealousy, Milrose Munce."

"Yeah, well, now that you've had that hallucination twice, it should strike you as characteristic, shouldn't it."

Arabella smiled a mysterious and lovely and annoying smile.

"You know, we really should be thinking about ways of getting to that door in the ceiling," said Milrose.

"Or, since that's impossible, we should be thinking of something else."

"Fine. Go ahead. You always did have the most humongodelicious imagination."

Arabella took this as the compliment that it was not intended to be.

And, miraculously, Milrose did think of something else. "I think I've got it. We're looking the wrong way. There are ghosts above us, yes, but there are also ghosts below!"

"You mean those grunting athletes in the basement? The ones who make, well, grunting noises whenever I walk by?"

"They're not exactly my fave species of lower primate either. And they're not hugely keen on me.

But I think there must be at least a couple of them with good hearts. Good, you know, aerobically swollen hearts. It's worth a try, perhaps."

"Except that the door is in the ceiling."

"True . . . Okay, so what about this," said Milrose Munce. "Jocks are generally a bit more courageous than poets."

"There is such a thing as intellectual courage, Milrose."

"Okay, they're not huge on that li'l attribute. But physical courage. That's kind of their forte. Right? So . . . maybe these guys don't have the same kind of cowardice when it comes to invading the first floor. Maybe they can swallow their fear and just do it."

"It would be nice, wouldn't it. To have all those large athletes whistling at me and snapping at me with wet towels."

"And saving you from Professional Help. Don't be such a snob."

"Well, I suppose I could suffer those indignities. Briefly."

"And maybe we could get them to hit Massimo Natica with a flying tackle, then toss him playfully in the air, so that he came down gently and gracefully upon the sharp end of the pitchfork, where he'd then sit for all eternity."

"See, Milrose? You do have a poetic soul."

This pronouncement, although clearly meant

ironically, nevertheless thrilled Milrose Munce. Of course, that was the route to Arabella's birthmark: to cultivate a poetic soul. He would then be irresistible.

"How," pondered Arabella, "are we to contact the helpful ghosts below? I suspect that none of my dear friends on the second floor will be capable of delivering the message."

"What with their yellow-bellied liver-quivering hyperventilating cowardice and all."

"That is not precisely what I meant."

"You know, I really think your deluded attachment to those bozos is preventing you from embracing our desperate, forbidden passion."

The silence following this remark was remarkable in its silenceness. Once again, Milrose Munce had watched his unbridled mouth screeching ahead of him down the track, as his mind flew into the dust like a wheel from a broken axle.

"You do have something of an imagination, don't you, Milrose Munce."

"Um, yeah. I mean, I don't know that it's totally desperate."

"That is not what I am saying."

"Right," said Milrose with no greater diplomacy, "I mean I'm only *imagining* that it's these bozos getting in the way. Could be something else."

"That too is a misinterpretation of my comment."

"Um, can we change the subject?"

"Always."

"Good. So which do you think it is? Desperate or forbidden? Or both?"

"That does not constitute a change in subject."

Milrose immediately recognized this. After saying it, of course.

"We were discussing the basement ghosts," said Arabella.

"Uh, yeah. Right. So how about those basement ghosts, anyway? Really something, aren't they."

"We were discussing how best to involve them in our rescue."

"Precisely. Now where were we?"

"That is where we were."

"Of course."

Milrose Munce was now thoroughly confused.

"It seems to me, Milrose, that we have two options. One is to have our friends on the second floor descend into the basement, where they can rally the ghosts there. That, however, would require them to pass the first floor, which is something they are not predisposed towards doing."

"Absolutely," said Milrose, who felt that his best course of action, until coherent thought returned, was simply to agree wholeheartedly with everything that Arabella said.

"A second possibility is to make contact with the basement occupants ourselves. Although this poses certain obstacles. Not the least of which is that they are insensitive to the scent of flowers."

"Maybe we could just pound on the floor with the blunt end of the pitchfork? That's the kind of noise they like, I bet."

"Except they'd have no idea what it meant."

"They'd probably just grunt and scratch their armpits with appreciation."

"Yes. Well, I suppose I could whisper seductively through the floor, in hopes of catching one of their hairy ears. That might inspire them to action."

"Sure. Great idea. Let's practise. Whisper something seductive to me, and I'll let you know whether it's working."

"Milrose, I do think you are rather out of control this evening." Arabella's hand fluttered, unconsciously, towards her heart, and Milrose wondered, with a sense of wonder, whether that approximate area hosted her glorious birthmark.

"Absolutely. Completely out of control. Couldn't have put it better myself."

The next couple of hours involved Arabella lying prone on the floor beside the bottom-most mattress, whispering seductive things into the linoleum.

Milrose Munce sat on that bottom-most bunk, trying his best to feign casual detachment, and stared at the girl lying so strangely at his feet.

Arabella was the sort who could make even the most ridiculous activity seem exotic and intriguing. It helped, noted Milrose, that she herself always looked both exotic and intriguing. Arabella's glowing red hair, barely discernible in the gloom (and where *was* that light coming from, anyway?), flowed without reason or definition across her frail shoulders, which featured twin sharp, pointy bits (blades?), and Milrose imagined that were he to place the index fingers of each hand, respectively, on each of those delicate extrusions, he would be electrified as if by a cattle prod, awoken to bliss and sent ecstatically through the ceiling, where he would—hmm—come face to face with Poisoned Percy.

At any rate, he found himself admiring her stretched form with unimpeded admiration. It was good, he thought, that she could not see the expression on his face. That expression portended, among other things, that Ms. Corduroy was no longer the object of his obsession, that this teacher had been replaced completely in the haze of his daydreams with the flaming peculiarity of Arabella, a peculiarity that in his mind was now the very definition of exquisition. A word that required defining.

He did his best to hear the contents of her seductive words, so that he could imagine them being directed, sincerely, at him. Unfortunately, the linoleum muffled them, so that all he heard was the abstract, undifferentiated sound of seduction. Which was not without its own pleasures, of course.

Arabella rolled over, in the most exquisite manner, utterly drained.

"Any success?"

"I do not know."

"I bet the linoleum has fallen in love with you."

"How kind."

"I mean it."

"You are the only boy I know who is capable of meaning the meaningless."

Milrose, who was not at his most alert, took this as a sincere and perhaps flirtatious compliment.

"I think we should sleep now," said Arabella. "Maybe this situation will all come clear in a dream."

"That only happens in stories."

"Nonsense. Things always come clear to me in dreams. Or I wouldn't bother to have them."

Upon announcing this, Arabella climbed into her own bunk, and soon a faint and feminine whistling snore ascended to tickle the ears of Milrose Munce.

For days Milrose and Arabella had been alone, if you discount the presence of Massimo Natica (which they did). Percy had not made further contact, and Arabella's crooning into the linoleum had failed to conjure any jocks. Furthermore, her dreams had clarified nothing—a disappointing fact, which Milrose was too kind to dwell upon.

Their increasing contempt for Massimo was now in danger of putting them in danger. Much as Milrose begrudgingly enjoyed this gloriously fruitless Help—for almost a week he had stood cheek to cheek with Arabella—he could not keep his demon tongue in check. Arabella too, perhaps because she had spent so much time with Milrose, had mastered her own form of virtuosic sarcasm. Hers was subtle, and while Milrose could generally detect it, Massimo Natica was less skilled in this regard, and all but the most blatant comments sailed well over his groomed head.

Certain comments, however, were inescapable. Arabella was continually offering Milrose graduate degrees whenever he pretended to accomplish something in the area of voice disposal. "Very impressive, Milrose. For that you deserve honours. I shall prepare your diploma this evening."

Whenever the words *diploma* or *fraud* were uttered, Massimo would respond in ways that were at first amusing and then less amusing. Recently he had taken to stroking the pitchfork handle, for instance, as if it were a beloved pet.

For the longest time Milrose and Arabella ignored these signals, so pleased were they that Massimo

Natica's bright facade was beginning to dim. His only truly effective technique—the uncanny ability to make them do whatever ridiculous thing he wished—was no longer quite so effective. Sometimes his hypnotic powers remained fully persuasive. More often, however, whenever they now slavishly followed his foolish suggestions, it was because they chose to for reasons of stealth or parody. Massimo Natica was still under the impression that he had undiminished magical power over his subjects.

Massimo did retain one crucial vestige of his former authority. Unfortunately, this was the *most* crucial. He still retained, in his pocket, the repulsively modern key. Nothing they could do in the way of subtle humiliation could compensate for this fact: they were locked in a den with Massimo Natica, his pitchfork, and his cattle prod.

Also unfortunate was that these tools had been joined by an equally distressing implement. One day when the words *fraud* and *diploma* were flying through the air in a thick flock, Massimo Natica had casually unlocked a cabinet set into the wall to reveal an object which—they hoped—also fell into the category of "antique."

It was an impressive medieval mace. Joined by a chain to an exquisitely crafted wooden handle was an iron ball, exquisitely studded with iron spikes. That this was not a modern mace, but clearly an artifact of an even more barbaric time, was indicated by the delicate patina of rust.

When they retired to their tower of beds, both Milrose and Arabella were thinking about very little but this mace.

"Actually, I've always been keen on medieval weapons," said Milrose, trying to put a bright face on things. He immediately regretted this flip remark when he noted that Arabella was in tears. Well, a single tear, which had taken up quivering residence on the vault of her nostril. "He will make us normal. He will succeed. I can see it. All of my efforts to make this world a peculiar place are in vain."

No, Milrose wanted to say. They are not at all in vain. They are increasing the portion of agonized happiness in this world, in ways you cannot even imagine. But what he in fact said was, "Darn."

Her hand fluttered to the left side of her stomach, five inches to the right of her navel, and Milrose of course wondered: could *this* be the site of what must be the world's most magnificent birthmark?

"I am beginning to despair, Milrose Munce."

"Oh man. Don't despair. That's all we need. It's your not despairing that is keeping me from despairing, and if the pair of us despair, we're toast."

Arabella's flower, which was—miraculously—still

alive and kicking, seemed to agree. It coughed, in a way that might easily be interpreted as a sob.

"I shall try to be strong," said Arabella.

"You *are* strong," said Milrose, silently adding "and exquisite, and mysterious, and on the verge of crushing my heart like a grape." For Milrose Munce was in fact *truly* developing, in his own awkward way, a poetic soul.

"The mace," said Milrose, in his most comforting tones. "I don't really think he intends to use it. Not in any, you know, physical way. It's a psychological thing. He's just saying: Look, I have a mace! It's not worth thinking about. Let's concentrate on getting out of here . . . you know, stuff that we can actually do something about."

"What can we do about it? Percy has not returned, and we're being threatened with antique weapons."

"We'll have to be resourceful."

"We have no resources."

Milrose examined his friend. "Arabella, this is unlike you. I miss your irrational confidence and hilarious self-possession."

She looked at the floor. "I'm sorry. I don't know what's gotten into me."

"I'm sure it's just temporary. You've been thrown off by a perfectly harmless medieval instrument of hideous carnage."

"I don't even know where to turn, what to begin to think about."

"It's quite simple, really, what we need: a brilliant plan. Surely you have one of those?"

"I am no longer a girl capable of brilliant plans."

"Arabella, I'm just not going to accept this. This is not *you*. This is not the many-splendoured Arabella whom I worship."

Did I really just say that? thought Milrose, aghast.

Did he really mean that? thought Arabella.

I must pretend I didn't say that, thought Milrose.

I must pretend I did not hear it, thought Arabella. On the other hand, thought Arabella, if I do not rouse myself from this cowardly despair, then I shall no longer have many splendours, and hence shall not be worshipped by Milrose Munce. Arabella, although she would never admit it to herself, much less to anyone else, did like being worshipped.

"I know what I am going to do," said Arabella, summoning absurd conviction. "I shall dream one up. A brilliant plan." She nodded, with absolute conviction, and her flower nodded too. "Yes, I'm overdue for a clarifying dream."

Milrose did not want to express his disappointment, now that Arabella was again hilariously self-possessed. Nevertheless, he found this strategy impractical, and felt that he had to say something. "Um, Arabella?" he said gently. "Can't you do better than that? This clarity/dreaming thing . . . I really don't believe it happens."

Arabella smiled. "That's because you don't believe."

"Well, yes. That's what I just said."

"So we agree. Good night, Milrose."

Arabella, once again armed with her boundless sense of a ludicrous ability to accomplish unrealistic things, returned to her bunk and closed her eyes.

As soon as she fell asleep, she found herself dreaming about a terrific battle. Warriors were arrayed in finery and armed with marvellous devices. Arabella stood on the edge of the fray, wondering at this gathering of forces. And then she fully grasped the nature of the meeting she had been called to witness: it was the Parent-Teacher Association. She woke up.

It was clear that this was one of those dreams that was supposed to be clarifying things. Unclear, however, was *what*. Which meant that the dream was particularly frustrating—a complete failure, and a disgrace to its genre. Still, she was heartened by the dream: it was, at the very least, strange and pregnant with meaning. Which indicated that she might soon be able to conjure a meaningful dream that actually meant something.

Milrose awoke in terror—not at the mace but at the remembrance of his "many-splendoured" comment the night before. This terror gave way to blinding embarrassed happiness, however, when he remembered that Arabella's response to the injudicious comment was not at all the tragic disaster that it might have been: if anything, the words had fully cured Arabella of her brief despair. Which meant that, despite his face-grabbing mortification, he could not regret having said them.

As a consequence of his unexpected bliss, Milrose found himself singing opera in the shower. He did not in fact *know* any opera, and his Italian did not exist, much less his German, but he sang it nevertheless, and his voice was—a surprise to both him and Arabella—not bad at all.

"For this must be the hour," sang Milrose Munce, "when angels haunt the shower / And lo my heart's great pain, would whirl down the drain / But I a mere shampoo, await the hair of you . . ."

This almost affecting aria was accompanied by the sympathetic gurgling of the drain. The song wafted across the den and into Arabella's receptive ears.

The gurgling of the drain was, in general, solid and predictable. You knew that the drain would gurgle; it was a constant. Hence it was surprising when that gurgle changed in tone. Milrose Munce was in the midst of improvising a ballad on the subject of cleanliness and its traditional relationship to godliness, when the gurgle of the drain grew suddenly very loud and annoying.

He stopped singing immediately. That annoying gurgle was familiar! Well, the gurgling aspect of it was not, but the annoyance surely was.

And then the drain coughed, and began to choke. "Munce," said the drain, in a truly irritating voice, "turn off that shower or I'm gonna drown . . ."

"Harry!" whispered Milrose with excitement. "Hurled Harry!"

"I'm going to hurl, all right, if you don't cut that water!"

Milrose immediately turned off the shower, and whispered into the drain, "Gotta whisper here, Harry. Our Professional Helper's lurking about."

"Gotcha."

"Great to hear your voice, man!" This was certainly the first time that Harry had ever heard these words. And probably the last. For his voice was capable of scraping warts from the tongue of a geriatric whale.

"Yeah, well, I told you I could probably do something about your situation. And you didn't believe me."

"O me of little faith. You're a hero, buddy. At least I think you are. What are you going to do?"

"Dunno yet. But some chick was cooing all sorts of seductive stuff from the floor above, and the jocks down here are all testosteroned up—I figure I can get them to do just about anything. Got any preference?"

"Oh man. Yeah. A daring rescue would rock, for instance."

"Right. Daring rescue. Can we be more specific?"

"Well . . ." said Milrose, biting his lip. "It may involve . . . in fact, it's *gonna* involve invading the first floor."

"Uh, right. First floor. Never been there. Uh, nice place?"

"Oh yes. Just like a tropical resort."

"We down here—well, the dead guys, anyway— have, um, misgivings about that floor."

"Entirely unnecessary. This place is heaven."

"But maybe some of the living lunkheads can put together a little invasion for you."

Milrose pondered this. Yes, that was true—the living jocks had no particular reason to fear the first floor. On the other hand, Milrose had—in the last minute or so—come up with at least three ingenious notions, all of which involved ghouls.

"Buddy, do this for me. Try. It's time you guys took back the first floor. It's *yours*, man. These jokers up here are *usurpers*. You gonna let them get away with that? I thought you guys were all about, you know, conquering the enemy."

"Well, beating the other team, actually . . ."

"*Exactly!* This is the other team we're talking about. Win this one for the Gipper! Go, ghouls!" (Who is the Gipper anyway? wondered Milrose Munce. Why is he so inspiring to jocks? Milrose decided that he would probably despise this Gipper, were he to meet him.)

Harry was silent. Clearly he was wrestling with his cowardice. And yet—and this is one of those rare impressive attributes you find inherent in athletes—Harry won. It took courage for a little guy to ride a horse that scared him (almost literally) to pieces, and that was the kind of thing that made it possible for Hurled Harry to contemplate the uncontemplatable. He was going to conquer the first floor.

"Consider it done."

"You're a prince."

"And I'm gonna bring an *army.*"

"You're a prince and a general!"

"We're gonna get you out of there, and we're gonna reclaim what is ours!"

"A prince, a general, and an orator!"

"Yeah, well, I'll do my best."

Milrose thought for a moment. "Um, look Harry. I know this isn't really your thing—hey, it's not *my* thing—but do you think you could get to the second floor? I sort of think you should launch the war from there. Believe it or not, I think we could use a poet in this battle."

"A *poet?*"

"Yeah, I know. Generally useless. But I think we can put this guy Percy to use in your military campaign. We've contacted him already, but he's dragging his feet. It's not going to be easy to get him fully on board. You might have to rough him up a bit."

"I like that idea."

"Thought you would. Okay, Harry, I gotta go. This is turning into kind of an epic shower, and our Helper is gonna get suspicious. Go, team!"

"Right on. I'll try to get back to you a few showers from now." He paused. "And, um, can you get the chick whispering again? Good for morale . . ."

"You got it."

Milrose Munce emerged into the den, hastily dressed and with his hair dripping. Massimo Natica, who was busy exchanging fraternal words with the medieval mace, had apparently noticed nothing.

Unfortunately, this was merely appearance. Massimo looked up from his conversation with the mace and made his way—still carrying his beloved weapon—towards Milrose Munce.

"Milrose," said Massimo, "were you having a conversation with a bar of soap?"

"Why yes I was," said Milrose after some hesitation. "Is there something wrong with that?"

Massimo was swinging the mace, casually, as if it were a purse. His smiling face, however, did not bear a casual smile. No, it was the sort of smile you associate with unstable soldiers who have become crazed after weeks in the jungle, naked except for a thick layer of giant mosquitoes.

"Something wrong?" said Massimo Natica, smiling and swinging. "Something *wrong*?"

Milrose and Arabella regarded each other with mutual hysterical terror.

"No, nothing *wrong*," said Massimo. "Nothing except the denial of *weeks* of Professional Help. The deliberate rejection of *weeks* of my Professional time. The undeniable *fact* of your *refusal* to *submit* to the *greatness* of my *expertise*."

"Now Massimo," said Milrose with a forced air of conviviality. "You know that's not true. I've made tremendous headway. Look how *rare* these conversations now are! You've almost cured me. So very close, man. If you give up now, you will be depriving yourself—and me—of your greatest Professional triumph! This will make the medical journals. The history books. The epic poems . . ."

Massimo did not look entirely convinced. He swung the mace with slightly less vigour now, but his smile retained a twinkle of malevolent madness, and he had developed a twitch in his neck.

"You are *trying* my Professional *patience*."

"I am, man. I'm trying my best. Let's give it one more try!"

Massimo let the mace hang limply at his side. His twitch began to calm itself, with longer and longer intervals between jerks. His smile began to take on an air of sanity.

"Breakfast," said Massimo with only slightly demented cheer.

After placing the mace on one of the comfy chairs—and Milrose made a note to avoid sitting on that chair without first clearing it of weaponry—Massimo walked almost steadily to the door. As always, that hideous brute was waiting behind the door, his tray laden with food. Milrose and Arabella had yet to set eyes upon that face, but they had mutually intuited a repulsive mug with disgusting eyes.

What perturbed Milrose Munce this morning—among many things, of course—was that the brutish arms of this silent servant now extended some *seven* inches past the cuffs of his medical shirt, and this indicated one of two possibilities. Either the shirt had shrunk (which Milrose desperately hoped was the case), or the arms had grown.

"Let us enjoy our breakfast this morning," said Massimo Natica. He did not add "as this may be our last occasion to do so on this earth," but Milrose detected the implication.

How Milrose missed ordinary life. He found that he even missed Mr. Borborygmus, that drooling idiot of a teacher. He would be happy, even, to lounge on the second floor, with Percy and poets. Or even in the basement, with Sledge. Okay, perhaps that was pushing it.

Still, his desires were definitely skewed. He desperately longed for Harry's grating voice in the grate at the foot of the shower, and Percival's pompous pronouncements through the ceiling above his bed. Neither of these could compete, of course, with the sound of Arabella whispering to the linoleum, but they did occupy a surprisingly prominent place in his daydreams.

Certainly the danger of the present situation was making the grass infinitely greener just about anywhere in the world. Milrose Munce could imagine a handful of prisons that might compete with the Den of Professional Help—in the Third World or Texas, for instance—but that was about it.

SEVEN

A WEEK PASSED—SEVEN SHOWERS IN TOTAL—
WITH NO WORD FROM HURLED HARRY. PERCY,
SURELY, WAS NOT TO BE RELIED UPON,
THOUGHT MILROSE, BUT HARRY WAS A DIFFER-
ENT ORDER OF GHOUL.

Milrose went to bed, on the seventh night, perturbed. His dreams were unpleasant. But he was
awakened by the sound of a magnificent explosion.
This was followed by chunks of ceiling falling
around and upon him, then fine plaster dust filling
his nostrils.

Of course, an explosion—especially one so very
close by—was always a welcome occurrence.
Moreover, it often signified, to Milrose, the proxim-
ity of a certain friend. "Dave?" he inquired.

"Greetings!" There was no mistaking that

demented voice. "I've been experimenting with temporary explosions. So far, so good, wouldn't you say?"

"Uh, aren't all explosions temporary?" asked Milrose. He sneezed.

"No. Not like this. I believe I have found a way to temporarily blow something up, so that it reverts to its unblown-up state in a couple of hours. We shall see, at any rate."

The loathsome yet welcome head of Dave was now fully visible, floating above in a cloud of plaster dust.

"That doesn't sound entirely possible, Dave," said Milrose, who was feeling a bit odd about having such a calm scientific discussion, given the circumstances.

"And yet it is. This is ghost chemistry, my friend. All sorts of new techniques. I've been researching—"

"Ah. Ghost chemistry."

"Known to the vulgar as 'magic.'"

"Man that's vulgar. 'Ghost chemistry' is vastly preferable."

"I in fact prefer the technical term: ectoplasmic manipulation. At any rate, yes. According to my calculations, we have a bit less than three hours of exploded ceiling, after which it goes back to being an unexploded ceiling."

"Marvellous. Thank you!"

"A pleasure."

"So, uh, what now?"

"An escape. Well, a temporary escape. You have to return, of course."

"Of course. Yes." Milrose thought for a moment. "Why?"

"Because I can get you out of here, but I can't get you out of the place I'm taking you to. And you'd probably prefer to be in the Den."

"Can't wait to see this place."

"Wish I could be more useful. But I've been doing a lot of research into this Help business as well—highly secretive stuff; nobody knows much about it—and it seems we dead guys are under a lot of constraints, when it comes to . . . interfering. Spells, counterspells . . . all very annoying. Now, we should get on with this, before my explosion deplodes—we've only got a couple of hours. Fetch the girl, and let's move."

Milrose climbed down the ladder until he was at Arabella's bed, where she was still engaged in a tiny, charming, fragile snore.

"Arabella . . ." Milrose whispered urgently. "Arabella!"

The delicate snore turned into a delicate snort, and then a delicate cough, followed by a delicate sneeze. "Milrose?"

"Yes! Come on up and meet my friend!"

"Your friend?" she asked, sleepily.

"You'll see. Come up to my bunk."

Arabella sat up and rubbed her eyes. She frowned and examined Milrose, to determine whether he was playing an elaborate joke. He did look sincere. "Okay. A . . . friend. All right. You go up. I'll follow."

Milrose scrambled up the ladder, and Arabella followed far more gracefully. When her head cleared his mattress, she was pleased to see a tremendous hole in the ceiling, framing the floating ex-body of that pyrotechnic prodigy, Deeply Damaged Dave.

Introductions were made, as Dave lowered a rope ladder through the hole. "Kind of low tech," he said, "but I wove it myself."

"Hey, it's a nice ladder," said Milrose.

"You did a lovely job, David," said Arabella.

"Thank you. Too bad you missed my temporary explosion."

"Aren't all explosions temporary?"

"He'll explain later. Dave, where are we going?"

"I'm not sure. A place with obscure and perhaps useful information, according to my research. I'd go myself, but it's one of those areas that's . . . off limits to the dead."

"Ah."

"Spells, counterspells, ingenious boobytraps, et cetera."

"How ingenious? Like, ingenious enough to snare a living kid?"

"Guess we'll find out. Come on up."

Milrose and Arabella climbed the rope ladder and scrambled awkwardly over the lip of the hole onto the floor above. Dave had not bothered to turn on any lights, and the second floor—whichever part they now occupied—was impenetrably dark.

Dave evaluated their chalk-dusted figures with his trained scientific eye, but did not seem to come to any conclusions. "So, when I got the message from your poet friend—man he's annoying—"

"Oh yes," said Milrose, "more annoying than friend."

"—I figured I better get personally involved. He doesn't seem like the most effective guy."

"Magnificent understatement. But hey: you should team up with my buddy Hurled Harry in the basement. He's potentially useful."

"The basement? Hm. Will ponder that. Contacting the basement is not trivial."

"He's keen."

"I'll look into it. We must get moving, however. I can't stick around for long—I'm really not supposed to be here. This, uh, temporary explosion . . . it's considered, technically, an assault on the first floor."

"For good reason."

"And we're expressly forbidden, you know, from using ectoplasmic manipulation against the first floor."

"Actually, I didn't know that."

"The enemy's got us pretty seriously tied down. I have to be back in the lab before this episode gets traced to me. And they have very sophisticated tracking methods."

"Ghost-sniffing dogs?" inquired Milrose.

"Something like that."

"Who are 'they'?" asked Arabella.

"It's complicated. And, uh, I can't talk about it. They know when they're being talked about. They can tune in the conversation and identify your precise location, and come at you with weapons too gruesome to be contemplated."

"Right. So let's change the subject."

It was difficult to know where precisely Dave led them when they set out from the site of his magnificent explosion. He insisted that they not turn on any lights, as this too would be an invitation to "them." Ghosts are quite good without light; living humans, however, tend to find it difficult to see.

"How are we expected to find our way back to the Den, Dave?"

"I think I have that covered."

"You *think*? What's the plan?"

"All shall be revealed."

"Sure hope so."

"Where precisely are we, David?"

"We are between the wall."

"Between the walls, you mean."

"No, between the wall. It's complicated. Involves turning left where you could never turn left before."

"Ah, that."

"Which takes you to a place, as far as we can determine, which is neither on one side of the wall nor the other, but between the wall."

"A lot more space between the wall than you'd expect."

"Yes. Nevertheless, you're not precisely *outside*. I can get you between the wall, but I can't get you to the other side. Or I'd have no trouble freeing you." Deeply Damage Dave shrugged apologetically. "And now," he said, "we are here."

"Here" did not seem like much of a place: it was a dead end. "This is a dead end," said Milrose. "But then, you're dead, so you probably approve."

"This," said Dave, "is the opportunity for another glorious if temporary disaster."

"Wonderful!" said Milrose, thrilled.

"Oh," said Arabella, worried.

"Watch," said Dave, intent.

He leaned forward in the darkness and placed both of his dead palms against the wall in front of them. (A wall between the walls, thought Milrose. All very confusing.)

When Dave removed his palms, the wall glowed phosphorescent blue where they had touched it: bright and ghostly handprints. He mumbled a few words.

"Is that Latin, David?" asked Arabella.

"Older," he said.

The words glowed in the air, just in front of the palmprints. Milrose and Arabella had never seen words glow before—neither of them had ever *seen* spoken words before, come to think of it—but there they were: mumbled expressions, in a language older than Latin, hovering in the air, quite visible.

Deeply Damaged Dave cleared his throat, as if to remind the hovering words that they had something to accomplish. Upon this hint, the words flowed into the handprints. It was like watching water from a tap enter a half-full sink, thought Milrose, thinking fondly of their aborted experiment with potassium. What followed was probably more exciting, even, than that experiment would have been if followed to its messy conclusion.

The handprints, as they filled with ancient words, began to grow. Slowly, they spread across and up the wall, like hand-shaped puddles of some glowing chemical. This was no ordinary chemical, Milrose knew from his profound experience of ordinary chemicals: must be a ghost chemical.

"Stand back," said Deeply Damaged Dave, in a voice that combined drama and pride: the voice of a suave magician.

They stood back.

The hands blew up.

Actually, they didn't so much blow up as in. Hand-shaped holes tore through the wall in front of them, but whatever had filled those holes exploded, conveniently, into the room on the other side: all Milrose and Arabella experienced was a percussive blast of air, accompanied by the appropriate noise.

"Nice," said Milrose.

"Very impressive, David," said Arabella.

They both clapped politely.

"Thank you. Thank you. Now, this is a slightly more temporary explosion: you have approximately two hours before the hole deplodes. Which is to say ex-explodes. Which is to say, fills back in, and entombs you, if you don't get out."

"Approximately?" said Milrose. "Can't you be more precise?"

"After further experimentation, I imagine I'll have the timing down to a science. This is a preliminary investigation."

"Ah. Which could, if we misjudge things, 'entomb' us."

"Yes. Might want to err on the side of caution."

"Gotcha." Milrose glanced at his watch. "And the other hole? In the ceiling?"

"Oh, that was a different chemical process. I had a bit more space to work with, and fewer concerns about collateral damage."

"You mean, killing us."

"Yes. I suspect you have at least two hours and fifteen minutes before the hole above your bed deplodes. Must be off now. Good luck."

"But," said Milrose.

There was no point in finishing the sentence, or even starting it properly, as Dave had vanished. Milrose looked at Arabella, and smiled weakly. He shrugged. And then he stepped through one of the hand-shaped holes in the wall in front of him. Arabella stepped through the other.

"Where are we, Milrose?"

"Interesting you think that *I* might be able to answer that question."

As their eyes adjusted, it became clear to both of them that they were in an enclosed space. Certain objects were glowing—not so much like the palm-prints but more like tired fireflies: pinpoints of dim light—and these were sufficient to illuminate the room. What these objects were, however, for the moment remained a mystery. As did the room itself.

The wall in front of them was one huge filing cabinet. It was filled from floor to ceiling with closed steel drawers. To either side were rough concrete walls, stained with damp.

The room had no windows. It also had no door. Luckily, it had temporary hand-shaped holes in the wall behind them, or there would be no possibility of exit. Which led both of them to wonder what kind of room this was. (The word *entombed* occurred to both of them, in fact.) Dave was right: even the Den of Professional Help seemed hospitable relative to this place.

Milrose decided to investigate. First he set out to determine precisely what was glowing. The light came from the drawers themselves. Each had a tiny bulb above the drawer's metal-framed label, and these bulbs all seemed on the verge of winking out completely. Some were a touch closer to death than others, but all were unhealthy. The feeble lights were, however, more than sufficient for him to make out what was written on the labels.

"Take a look at this, Arabella . . ."

The labels were not comforting. Oh no. They purveyed the opposite of comfort, which in this case was a heady mixture of confusion, nausea, angst, and that mysterious impulse which makes hunters want to kill moose.

"Helped: Jan. 1–Mar. 31, 1972."

"Helped: Apr. 1–Jun. 31, 1972."

"Helped: Jul. 1–Sep. 31, 1972."

Etc.

Milrose had no doubt that the Help to which these labels referred was of the Professional variety.

Arabella was squinting at another group of labels, and had come to a similar conclusion. "Milrose, I think we're in some kind of archive."

"Yes . . . the collected documents relating to decades of horror inspired by Professional Help."

"Try to be a little less pessimistic, Milrose."

"Does this look like a jolly archive to you?"

"Appearances can be deceiving."

"Yeah, well, while we're throwing about hackneyed phrases, sometimes what you see is what you get."

"Let's not argue, shall we. If something terrible happens, then I'll grant your argument."

"Great. I hope something really slitheringly horrible happens. So I win."

Although he wasn't entirely keen to, Milrose opened one of the drawers. In fact, he opened the very last drawer: in the bottom corner on his right. Why this drawer? Well, it helped that as he was trying to decide which to open, the light above this drawer's label began to flicker, then grew bright, then flickered, then went out. As he approached, it flickered again. The drawer was clearly teasing him. It was behaving like a coy firefly. None of the other drawers was going to nearly so much trouble to catch his attention. Moreover, it had a different designation than the others: instead of "Helped" and a date, the label read "Pending."

"What's in there?"

"I don't know . . . it's slithering and it's horrible . . ."

"Is it?"

"Just kidding. It's a bunch of file folders."

One of these file folders seemed most anxious to be consulted, as it kept bobbing up and down, flirtatiously. Milrose began to reach for this folder, and it obliged by sliding—of its own accord—up and out from between the others and finding its way into his hand.

"Hm," said Milrose. "Slithering file folders."

"But not horrible . . ."

"No, not yet."

Arabella stood cautiously at his shoulder as Milrose examined the eager file. The folder was of the usual bland manila, with a tab on the top left to identify the contents. On this tab was printed a name, in handwriting that seemed to Milrose not entirely under control—as if the writer were in the midst of a psychotic break, or perhaps a fierce battle with armed opponents: "Milrose Bysshe Munce."

"Your middle name is *Bysshe*?"

Milrose blushed so deeply that he glowed like a palmprint. "Er, I don't use it much."

"It's lovely."

"It's appalling. But thank you."

Milrose opened his folder with hands that shook only slightly, but enough to ensure that the papers within fell onto the floor in a complex mess. Arabella calmly sat on the floor and collected the pages. Milrose got down on his knees beside her, less calmly, and together they began to examine the file. The light was not good, but their eyes were becoming accustomed to it, and they found themselves capable of reading if they squinted.

Much documentation had been devoted to the case of Milrose Bysshe Munce. Dozens of sheets of closely lined paper had been entirely filled, by hand, with observations. Milrose recognized the same jittery—actually, mad—handwriting that had scrawled the name on the folder.

Because they had a limited amount of time before they were entombed, Milrose and Arabella skipped randomly through the pages, intending in this way to arrive quickly at a deep understanding concerning the case of Milrose Bysshe Munce.

And because random skipping is not the best path to wisdom, they did not quite succeed. Also, the notes were not entirely coherent. It was easy to imagine the author, in fact, foaming at the mouth and howling at his pen while writing. But they did glean a few crucial points. Milrose discovered that he was—according to this report—a student widely revered by the student population, and widely feared by the staff. He was a "natural-born leader," according to one note, which made him a "danger to the educational harmony of the school." He was also, according to one loony note, a "sarcastic hero." Most of this was news to Milrose. But then, the person who had written these notes was clearly insane.

The crazed author had also made one very sane and somewhat disconcerting observation. He/she/it knew, quite clearly, that Milrose Munce was conversant with the dead.

An hour later, Milrose and Arabella were still sitting on the damp floor of the archive, and were now surrounded by a messy heap of file folders. They had frantically searched each of the drawers, looking for information that might prove useful. Arabella's file had been right behind Milrose Munce's, and had been approximately as informative. Again, however, one salient fact stood out: the mad author knew, ominously, that Arabella was on friendly terms with the dead.

They had immediately wondered whether seeing ghosts was an attribute shared by any of the other students on file. They had opened drawers and searched randomly through different folders and found—to their excitement and dismay—that in fact *all* of the students they looked into seemed to have this in common. Admittedly, they had not had time to go through more than a portion of the cases, but it was eerie to note this common theme. Both Milrose and Arabella strongly suspected that were they to go through every folder, they would probably find that every one of these Helped individuals had been intimate with the world of the dead.

All of the folders they examined said much the same thing. A student had been deemed a candidate for Help. He or she had been admitted to the Den. The daily reports regarding the weeks following this were mostly dull and uninformative, consisting of statements like: "Today patient made no substantial progress towards socialization. On the Wickter Scale of Normalcy, patient has still barely progressed beyond 6.2, which is unacceptable." The last page of every file (except their own) ended abruptly with: "Patient cured."

This cure was always abrupt. In fact, the cure always seemed to take place precisely forty-two days after the patient had been admitted into Help. Generally the patient had made little or no progress on the Wickter scale—and had often worsened—yet six weeks after commencement, each patient was suddenly "cured," and the file terminated.

"I don't like this curing business," said Milrose.

"Neither do I," said Arabella.

"It doesn't seem . . . positive."

"No."

"I mean, nobody ever gets actually Helped all that much, do they? Not according to the Wickter Scale."

"I do not like that scale."

"And then they're suddenly cured."

Both were thinking much the same thing. And that thing was close enough to the word *entombed* that it made them suddenly anxious to return to the Den before the wall deploded.

Deeply Damaged Dave had indeed provided for their return. It was difficult to lose their way, given Dave's helpful (if somewhat extreme) navigational aids. He had arranged a series of (probably temporary) explosions, which occurred, one after another, every few minutes, to guide them in the proper direction. Just as they were becoming perplexed—as stumbling in the dark so often renders one—a bright flash and matching bang would ignite in the near distance, indicating where they ought to go next. (Dave counted on Milrose being one of those few people who make their way *towards* explosions.)

In this intermittently dramatic manner—every explosion caused them to flinch, if not jump—they at last found their way back to the hole in the floor, beneath which could be glimpsed the tower of beds.

The rope ladder had disappeared: could Dave have neglected this one detail, after being so careful with his pyrotechnics? But the topmost bed was not very far below, so they counted to three and jumped.

They landed with a soft sproing. A mere second later they heard a noise that can only be called the opposite of an explosion (if you've never heard this noise, then you can't really grasp how strange it is), and the ceiling deploded. Which is to say, all the bits of plaster lying on the bed beside them shot through the air to find their former places in the former ceiling; the plaster dust whooshed back into the places between those places; and the ceiling quickly became solid and whole and unexploded. It was impressive, if a touch unsettling—had they taken a second more to find their way back, or had counted to four before jumping, then they would never have been able to return to the den.

"I suppose we made it back in the nick of time." Milrose stopped to ponder this. "What do they mean by 'the nick,' anyway?"

As breakfast was fast approaching, there seemed no point in going back to bed. Milrose and Arabella sat upon the bunk and tried to make sense of the evening's adventure.

"I think this evening has been helpful," said Arabella.

"You're right: we learned helpful stuff. Dave will be pleased with our research."

"What precisely have we learned, do you think?"

"Um . . ." Milrose turned this over in his mind. "Well . . . I guess we know that people get sentenced to Help for seeing ghosts."

"We do not really know that. All we know is that everyone sentenced to Help *does* see ghosts. We have no proof that this is *why* they are sent here. And we can't really speak for everyone. We didn't read all the files."

"You're nitpicking."

"One of us has to."

"Why? And what's a nit?"

"I think it's a small bug."

"Well," said Milrose, "you keep picking small bugs. (What does that *mean*?) And I'll continue to assume that everyone is sent here precisely because they see ghosts. In fact, I bet they do this to everyone who shows that ability. I mean, you and I are the only people I know who are aware of our dead friends, and guess what: we're in Help."

"I'll grant you that."

"And I think it's safe to say that Help is designed to cure this condition. Not simply the hearing of supposedly non-existent voices. The actual seeing of ghosts."

"Okay. That is in fact borne out by the files."

"And, furthermore, it's pretty clear that Help is completely useless in that respect. All the files seemed to suggest that patients kept up their conversations with the dead, no matter what was done to them."

"Until they got . . . cured."

"Yes."

They both shuddered.

"Let's see," said Milrose, veering away from that gruesome subject. "We also know a bit more about why they're concerned about *us*, in particular."

"I don't think we know anything useful."

"Well, apparently I'm a born leader. That's something. Whoever wrote my file seemed particularly annoyed by that."

"True. Frightened, even. You're a 'danger.'"

"Who knew," said Milrose. "Of course, I've never led anyone anywhere in my life."

"If you were born to lead, you have lots of time to start. I'm sure many people start leading later in life."

"Thank you. And I like to think of myself as a danger."

"Of course."

"I bet we're *both* dangers."

"Do you think so?"

They stopped speaking in order to briefly enjoy that thought.

"Um, Arabella? Speaking of . . . well, danger . . . how many days have we been in Help?"

She started counting on her fingers. "About thirty-six."

"About? I suspect we want an exact number."

"I'm not good with numbers."

"Because the files are kind of unwavering when it comes to the date of the cure. Forty-two days and you're done."

"I'm almost sure it's thirty-six."

"Then I'm almost sure we're gonna be cured six days from now."

They lapsed into an unhappy silence, as neither could think of anything much to say. Among the many things in the world they did not desire, this was now chief: they did not want to be cured.

EIGHT

ONE DISTRESSING ASPECT OF MASSIMO
NATICA'S DECLINE WAS THE GROWING INCO-
HERENCE OF HIS THERAPEUTIC STRATEGIES.
WHILE ONCE MERELY SILLY AND INEFFECTIVE,
WHAT MASSIMO WAS HAVING THEM DO NOW
WAS MORE IN THE LINE OF DANGEROUS AND
UNPRINCIPLED.

"I sense that you do not trust me," said Massimo
Natica over breakfast. This was perhaps his first
truly accurate observation.

"Aw, Massimo. How could you possibly come to
such a depressing conclusion?"

Natica ignored Milrose, as if that last remark were
somehow not sincere. "This is not normal. *Normal*
children trust adults in positions of authority. So, we
are going to work on this. Trust." He smiled one of

his least appetizing smiles. "Now, before you trust me, you must learn to trust each other."

"But we already do," said Milrose.

"We shall see," said Massimo Natica.

In order to ensure that Milrose and Arabella were not abnormally suspicious of each other, they were now to engage in exercises devoted to "interpersonal trust." Milrose had heard of such exercises, which were popular in drama classes: a blindfolded actor would tilt forward, so that—if not caught by a fellow student—he would plant his face fully and painfully in the floor. This was meant to instill trust between students. You simply *expected* your fellow actor to catch you before you crushed your nose. Sometimes these experiments could become fraught with something less than trust: if, for instance, the guy who was supposed to catch you was also competing with you for the lead in the next play. Or, worse, the catcher had an eye on your girlfriend, and considered you the major obstacle to his romantic ambitions. Still, incidents of serious nasal impact were rare.

What Massimo was proposing, however, involved a considerable element of luck on top of the usual trust. Arabella was made to stand blindfolded against the one blank wall, while Milrose—also blindfolded—was made to rush at the wall, as if jousting, with the pitchfork held in front of him like a lance. Arabella was to trust that Milrose would plant the pitchfork into the wall instead of into her.

Milrose did his very best not to impale Arabella on the end of his pitchfork, and Arabella did her very best not to be run through like a kebab, but neither could *guarantee* that this would not happen, no matter how deeply went their trust.

Of course, they did in fact trust each other deeply. And one positive consequence of this exercise—the *only* positive aspect—was that they seemed to bond further as they courted Arabella's inadvertent murder. It was, in a truly sick and beautiful way, romantic.

Now you might of course wonder *why* Milrose and Arabella would allow themselves to be caught up in such an exercise. Unfortunately, Massimo's powers of persuasion had not left him entirely, and when he *truly wished* for them to undergo a certain technique, they really had no choice in the matter. Massimo Natica could no longer pull this off consistently, but when manic obsession entered the picture, his talents returned. And he really, really wanted to witness this exercise in trust.

It became, to be precise, more of an exercise in prayer and strategy. Prayer for obvious reasons. Milrose Munce had never considered himself particularly religious, but he found himself praying with astonishing sincerity that he not be the cause of Arabella's violent demise. Her death under any circumstances would have driven him to an eternity of grief. Her death at his hands, however, would be infinitely worse. Truly bad, with no redeeming features whatsoever. Hence he prayed.

Her prayers were surprisingly different. You'd imagine that she'd focus mostly upon being run through like a quail on a spit—that her prayers would run along the lines of, "Please, Lord, let me not be skewered by a pitchfork." Arabella's prayers, however, were far more complex. For she cared mostly that her ghosthood not come at the hand and fork of Milrose Munce, simply because of the wilderness of eternal anguish it would cause him. If prayers are answered, even in the Den of Professional Help, it may well be for this strange reason: there was very little selfish in Arabella's sincere wish to remain unpierced.

Strategy was the other main deterrent to the addition of yet one more kebab to this world. Milrose Munce would always indicate that he was about to set himself into motion by pawing the floor loudly with his foot, like a bull about to charge. Arabella, upon hearing this sound, would emit a subtle "eep," which set in motion a sort of echolocation, so that Milrose might triangulate like a bat and aim in any other direction than eep-ward. This was the soundtrack to that operatic exercise in trust: paw, eep, gallop, thud. Perhaps more "thoock" than "thud," as the tines of the pitchfork would penetrate an inch or so into the wall.

Massimo watched with satisfaction.

That night, both had an inordinately difficult time getting to sleep—a consequence of terror—but once they succeeded, Arabella had a clarifying dream. It was about time. Unfortunately, upon waking, she could not remember it.

Arabella had a technique to deal with this, however. She closed her eyes and pretended that she was in fact asleep, and this, predictably, tricked the dream into coming back, like an abandoned dog, to nuzzle her eyeball.

And there she was again, vividly, in a full-length faux-ermine robe and a magnificent tiara (adornments she had barely noticed in the dream, as this was hardly unusual clothing); she was making a stately progress down the corridor of the dank, mushroomous basement. To either side were athletes, awed by her presence in their midst—they had briefly stopped giving each other wedgies; their bleating had diminished to a low snuffling murmur—and at the end of the corridor was a creature in a cage.

This was no ordinary creature. He was, perhaps, human, except that his forehead was so low as to barely exist: it was just tall enough to entertain eyebrows, and these brute ornaments blended almost with the hair on his head. His nose was unlike most human noses, in that it had no definite shape: it was a sort of doorknob of cartilage, dominating the centre of his simian face. The neck, too, was simian, if in fact a bit wide relative to the neck of the average gorilla. And even the most vicious of the great apes had eyes displaying more warmth and intelligence than those glaring from above that blasted nose and behind those pitiless bars.

Arabella made her regal way between the ranks of sombre athletes towards this appalling beast. She held a key in her hand. And she realized, as she examined the dream, that she fully intended to use this key to free the monster from his cage.

It all makes sense, thought Arabella, upon opening her eyes. Although she could not figure out precisely what kind of sense it made, she was pleased to know that everything was now clear. After yawning, she shook her head to rid it of cobwebs (Arabella was not sure that her head contained actual cobwebs, but it seemed best to play it safe), and climbed the tower of beds to where Milrose was snoring. She poked him gracefully in the ribs. "Milrose!" she whispered.

He opened one eye, annoyed.

"Milrose Munce, I have had a clarifying dream!"

He closed the eye, and sighed. "Okay, let's hear it."

"You have to have more faith in my dream. Or I shall not tell it to you."

"Fine. I'm thrilled that everything has come clear to you in your sleep. Dying to hear it. Really. Now tell me all."

Arabella, although she was not at all fooled by this weary pledge of fascination, told him the dream anyway. When she finished, she noticed that Milrose was staring at her with amused disbelief.

"Arabella, that is the least clarifying dream I have ever heard."

"I disagree. You just have a bad attitude."

"But what has become clear?"

"I have no idea."

"For this you woke me up . . ." Milrose turned away from Arabella, in fond annoyance. Then he suddenly perked up. "Hang on. You say he had a nose like a doorknob, this creature?"

"Yes. Precisely."

"And his neck—was it . . . thicker than the average neck?"

"Oh, a tree trunk."

"What about his forehead. Would you say that he had a *tall* forehead?"

"It was the least tall forehead I have ever encountered. It barely deserved the title 'forehead.' In fact, it's only out of generosity that I'm calling that whole bulbous thing a head."

"Sledge!" said Milrose.

"I beg your pardon?"

"You dreamed about Sledge! He's a borderline psychopath. Lives in the basement."

"He *lives* there?"

"Well, he hangs out there. Athlete. Football player. Squarebacker or something. Nobody else could possibly fit that description." Milrose thought for a moment. "Yes, this is a truly exceptional dream, Arabella. Sledge—I never thought about this before—Sledge is a survivor of *Professional Help*."

"What? He wasn't 'cured'?"

"Apparently not. I wonder if that makes him unique. But he definitely had Help. Meaning that, insofar as he's aware of anything, he must be aware of our dead friends."

"We have something *in common* with this brute?"

"Yup. Who knew. Moreover, I suspect he is on our side. I mean, when I had my last conversation with him—ha! 'conversation'—it was pretty clear that he didn't have fond memories. Of Help."

"So that's why I must free him!"

"Precisely! Superb dream."

"Thank you."

"Free him from what?"

"The cage."

"Yes, but what cage?"

"That's all I know."

"Well, let's get on it, then."

Getting on it proved less difficult than might have been imagined. Getting on it would, they both supposed, involve descending into the basement. Hence it was with some excitement that Milrose noticed something dangling from the ceiling.

"What is that?" said Arabella, who had also noticed this dangling object.

"A chemistry set!" said Milrose, who had seen more than a few in his time. "A nice one! And it seems to be very old."

The set was one of those jaunty children's toys, in a suitcase-like metal box upon which was painted a cheerful boy genius about to wreak havoc with some liquid in a test tube. Milrose had inherited just such a chemistry set from his grandfather, and before blowing it up during an unfortunate (but thrilling) experiment, had learned a great deal from it. The nice thing about antique chemistry sets is that they contained all sorts of astonishingly dangerous chemicals later deemed inappropriate for children.

The suitcase was hanging from a rope, and the rope itself was familiar: it was the same homespun ghost stuff out of which Dave had woven his rope ladder to help them climb through the deploded ceiling. This rope seemed to descend through the floor, without actually piercing it, much as a ghost's arm might emerge from a solid object (an ordinary occurrence they had both witnessed on many occasions).

"A present from Dave!" said Milrose. "Most excellent."

Milrose, with Arabella supporting him so that he did not fall from the hideous height, stood on the bunk and leaned out to untie the chemistry set from its rope. Upon closer examination, it showed further Dave-like characteristics. Where the old metal box had said "Chemistry," Dave had augmented this word, in nicely embossed and painted letters, so that it read "Ghost Chemistry." In full, the box now promised "Ghost Chemistry Set for the Young Inquiring Mind. Educational! Fun! Unfold the Mysteries of the Immaterial World!" Milrose looked closely, and yes: it had once read "Material World." The painted boy genius staring gleefully at the glowing test tube had a familiar expression: cheerful obsession, bordering on insanity.

As Milrose opened the metal box, Arabella noted that he had much the same expression on his face.

The ingredients featured in the Ghost Chemistry Set were not at all like the bits and pieces purveyed by the antique set Milrose had inherited. The vials contained things that might have been called chemicals, except that they had eyes, and were very much alive. The test tubes and flasks and devices were more complicated than the ones Milrose had shattered at home: one bottle had no inside and no outside; the test tubes had—was it possible?—teeth; the rubber stoppers beat like tiny hearts.

To explain all this, the set included a manual, but it was unlike any textbook Milrose had ever encountered. First of all, it was handwritten, in golden ink that glowed and moved restlessly on the page. From the start, it did not much resemble a chemistry book, in that it concentrated mostly on the pronunciation of difficult words in a language Milrose could not identify.

"This is gonna involve some study," he said.

"Lovely," said Arabella. "You shall study, and I shall sleep." She yawned, covering her mouth with a pretty hand, and turned to crawl down the ladder.

Milrose turned to the manual, and focused his clever mind, fiercely, on the longest and probably most useful chapter: "The Art of Temporary Explosions, as Revealed Through the Careful Explorations and Experimental Activities of Deeply Damaged Dave, Scientist."

The next day's Help was a nauseating blur for Milrose, as he had not slept at all after being woken by Arabella. He had spent the entire night studying ghost chemistry, and had learned a great deal, but his brain had ceased to function sometime during breakfast and was now about as sentient and useful as a spleen. The only bit of information to pierce his mental haze was the announcement that Massimo would be away Friday, to attend a special session of something or other to which he had been invited as an important something and was expected to do something important. The details were foggy, but it was obvious that Massimo was lying: the word *important* simply did not ring true when applied to Massimo Natica. Nevertheless, he was going to be away, on Friday. Two days from now.

Massimo had decided to experiment for a few days with exercises devoted to virtues other than trust, and this was a major blessing: if Milrose had been forced to practise trust in his mentally diminished state, it is not likely that Arabella would have remained unforked for long.

At last Help drew to a close, and dinner was eaten, and Massimo departed for whatever loathsome place he occupied when he was not being a great Professional. The excitement Milrose felt at having the opportunity to return to his studies banished all blur, and his mind again focused on the task at hand.

"How are we doing, Milrose?" asked Arabella, impressed with the scholarly intensity Milrose brought to this project.

"Good. Excellent. Yes. Figuring it all out. Yup. Too bad none of it works."

"Sorry?"

"Well, I did some elementary chemistry last night—and I'm pretty sure I got it all correct, the pronunciation and whatnot—but nothing happened."

"That's not a good sign."

"No. But this stuff *is* fascinating."

"That may well be, but we have important things to accomplish. Don't you think you can get it to . . . well, accomplish something?"

"Hard to say. It sure *sounds* like effective stuff. I'm going to try something more ambitious tonight. We'll see."

Arabella watched with interest as Milrose arranged the chemicals on the floor beneath the tower of beds. They were adorable, these chemicals: they would shyly bat their eyelashes at each other and hide in the corners, and occasionally make small sighing noises. Milrose would place one in the bottle that had no inside and no outside, and the chemical would become confused; he would then intone something magisterial in the unknown language, and the chemical would cringe in awe; after which there would be a long, dramatic pause, at the end of which . . . nothing happened.

Ghost chemistry, although impressive, was really not very useful. Not in the hands of Milrose Munce, at any rate. "Perhaps you have to be a ghost," mused Milrose. "Perhaps I ought to be dead."

"Please don't die," said Arabella, in an unusually urgent tone of voice, which Milrose noted with satisfaction.

The only perceptible change wrought by this chemistry was a renewed vigour on the part of Arabella's flower, which seemed once again determined to be the most florid thing ever to floresce. Milrose, if nothing else, had conjured an overwhelming scent of almonds. That, however, was not going to free Sledge from his cage—assuming that this was what they were meant to accomplish.

The next morning, Milrose was not only in a blur but also in something like despair. Again he had not slept, and again he had learned a great deal, and again he had managed to achieve nothing.

According to Arabella's calculations, today was their thirty-eighth day in Professional Help. Neither liked to talk about it, but for a long time both had been very much aware of the coming Monday, and what it meant. Monday would be the forty-second day. On Monday, if the general rule held true, they were going to be cured.

Even if Milrose weren't desperately tired, he would have been miserable. But fatigue meant that he was both miserable and half comatose. He looked forward to the morning's shower as salvation: his last hope of remaining conscious for the rest of the day.

The shower did prove a form of salvation, but in ways Milrose had not expected.

"Psst," said the drain.

Milrose dropped the soap. "Beg your pardon?"

"I said 'psst,'" said the drain, in a very Harry-like voice, "and what I meant was, turn off the water or I'm gonna drown."

"How can a ghost drown?" said Milrose. "Meant to ask you that before."

"Complicated. Forget it. Concentrate. Did you get the chemistry set?"

"Yeah. It's great. Doesn't do a thing, though."

"Oh, it will. Just make sure you learn the stuff."

"Learning away. What do you mean, 'it will'?"

"You'll find out soon enough. I suggest you make tomorrow a chemistry day."

"You know, you guys with all your hints and half-revealed truths are getting really annoying."

"Can't be helped. Spells, counterspells, heat-seeking missiles . . ."

"Yeah, yeah. Know all about it. So you've been in touch with Dave?"

"Sure have. Love that guy. Sure knows how to put on a show."

"No kidding. You've met, then?"

"Naw . . . he's on the third floor. But he sends these fire-breathing messages to the basement. Awesome stuff—I'll tell you all about it later. Suffice it to say, man, we're joining forces. Everyone's joining forces. It's gonna be one big fat force, dude."

"Brilliant."

"So, tomorrow. Chemistry. Make it a priority."

"Shouldn't be a problem. Massimo's away."

"I know."

"Oh."

"Turn on the water again—this is gonna look suspicious. I gotta go."

And with that, Harry's voice departed, and a great cloud of sonic irritation was lifted from the atmosphere.

Arabella was excited to learn of Harry's reappearance. She was disappointed to hear that he hadn't said much that was concrete or useful, but they were both getting used to this. It was decided that Milrose would complete his studies early in the evening and get at least some sleep for the day ahead: Friday, a day without Massimo.

By now, Milrose had almost memorized the entire chemistry manual. He really was quite good at studying things, if they were things worth studying. By the time he was ready for bed, Milrose felt that he had a knowledge of temporary explosion far surpassing that of any mortal (given that no mortal had ever studied the matter, this was highly likely), and that his wisdom might even be approaching that of the great pioneering scientist in the realm, Deeply Damaged Dave.

———

"Is this Friday the thirteenth, by any chance?" asked Arabella, stretching.

"Nerp. The twenty-second. Anyway, I've always felt that Friday the thirteenth was a fraudulent concept."

"Me too. Yes. Perhaps the twenty-second, however, is truly potent."

"Yeah. Extremely unlucky. Especially if you happen to be, say, a Professional Helper."

"I feel this to be the case."

"Good. You've always had unerring intuition." Milrose frowned. "God, I sound like Percy."

"You should be pleased," said Arabella happily. "It is further proof that you are developing a poetic soul."

"I'd rather develop a huge wart between my eyes," said Milrose, pleased.

Breakfast was waiting for them on a tray in front of the door. Whenever Massimo was away, that was how their food arrived, although they had never managed to catch the delivery man in the act of delivering. This was for the best: they agreed he would have unnervingly long and disgusting arms, which would doubtless affect their appetites.

Milrose and Arabella ate quickly, as both were very much in the mood to see whether Harry's vague prediction was at all valid. Apparently, the chemicals were in a similar mood: when Milrose opened the chemistry set, they were jiggling and bouncing, and their tiny eyes were smiling.

When placed on the floor, this time, the cheerful chemicals lined up expectantly, their eyes fixed upon Milrose. He arranged a few toothy test tubes about them and placed the insideless bottle off to one side.

"Right," said Milrose. "Stand back!" This was to Arabella, who was sitting on a bunk some levels above, but "stand back" is what great magicians and scientists say when about to accomplish momentous things. He then proceeded, in his very best accent, to intone potent words from the manual in a weird incantation, which the chemicals seemed to particularly enjoy. They bobbed up and down and glanced at each other in flushed appreciation—isn't that lovely, that incantation?—and blew up.

The explosion was certainly at least as fine as what Dave had accomplished with the ceiling. If anything it was more precise and elegant. Milrose had produced an almost perfectly circular hole in the floor.

"Exquisite," said Arabella.

"Thank you. Tell me this doesn't make poetry look totally lame by comparison."

"Perhaps this is a form of poetry."

"Yes. You're right. It is. I can't wait to present Percy with one of my poems."

"Munce," said a noxious voice from below. "You there? Munce!"

"Harry! Yes, yes—please, not so annoying! I mean, not so loud."

"Nice explosion. Now get down here. There's work to be done."

Milrose peered through the hole: Harry had helpfully put a stepladder beneath the hole and was standing beside it.

"All prepared, are we, Harry?" said Milrose, testing the ladder with his hand before descending.

"You have no idea. Buddy, there've been wars—world wars—that didn't have this kind of preparation behind them. I am nothing if not prepared. Triple redundancy."

"Go, team."

"Say. Whatever happened to that chick who was chatting up our ceiling?"

"She would be right here," said Arabella with a hint of revulsion. Her face was framed by the lovely circular hole.

"Ah. Great! Hi, chick. I mean, greetings, fair maiden. Oh hell, whatever."

"Hello, Harold. A pleasure."

Arabella made her delicate way down the ladder. She stood beside Milrose, and both of them stared about. It did not look much like the basement they had encountered before. They were in a long, bleak corridor of stained concrete. No lockers were in evidence, and no athletes, with one notable exception: Sledge was imprisoned, much to his psychotic consternation, in a powerful steel cage in the centre of the floor.

Milrose, although hardly fond of the linebacker, was appalled to see Arabella's dream so brutally realized. "Look what they've done to Sledge!"

"Actually, *I* did it," said Harry.

"Oh."

"Yeah. What do you think of the cage? Some of the dead jocks are crack welders—spend most of their time on muscle cars. Not much else to do." He added with a touch of pride: "I designed it myself."

"Swell."

Sledge, on the other hand, clearly did not appreciate Harry's designer cage. He roared, meaningfully, and fixed his blunt eyes on Harry's crushed skull. As if he intended to crush it.

"Um, Harold?" asked Arabella politely. "Is there any reason why you have that handsome athlete in a cage?"

"Oh yeah. Sure is. Makes him angry, you see."

"I do see."

"And we want him good and angry. And he's kind of dangerous, uncaged."

"Also apparent."

"So, when we get him seriously angry, and need him dangerous, we'll let him out."

"Thank you for the explanation."

"No prob," said Harry, gallantly. "So, uh, you got a name, chick?"

"Arabella Smith," said Arabella.

"Your last name's *Smith*?" said Milrose, suppressing a grand mal seizure.

"It is," said Arabella, with a failed attempt at pride.

"Cool," said Harry, who hadn't the slightest sense of how earth-quivering this revelation truly was.

"Where are we, Harold?"

"Ah. Complicated matter, that. We're in the basement, but . . . we're between the wall."

"Not so complicated," said Milrose, trying to maintain his poise while reeling in the wake of Arabella's casual name-drop. "Been there, done that."

"Oh. Well, it's new to me. I've never been between the wall. Your buddy Dave told me how to get here."

"How is it again that you guys are in contact? What with all the floors between you and all?"

"Oh yeah. Inspired guy, that Dave. He has this burning-bush routine. You know the little clumps of fungus that grow in the shower?"

"Sadly, yes."

"He makes them catch fire and speak. Great method of communication. Biblical, almost."

"Love it. So, uh, I take it we're here—between the basement wall—for a reason?"

"Oh yeah. *Oh* yeah."

"Preferably a reason intimately connected to our glorious escape from the den?"

"That and better. Come with me. I'll fill you in on the way."

Milrose accompanied Hurled Harry down the oppressive corridor. Arabella had been left behind to manage Sledge. (Harry had read somewhere that vicious beasts could be rendered briefly docile by the presence of a chick.) The corridor was brighter than the place between the wall on the second floor, but just barely—and Milrose could not figure out where the light was coming from.

As they advanced, Harry lowered his repulsive voice, until he was whispering directly into the ear of Milrose Munce. Harry's whisper had all the quiet grace of an industrial staple gun.

"Don't want them overhearing. I mean, they're horribly busy, so it's not a huge issue."

"Who's 'they,' and what are they busy doing?"

"They are hideous warriors, brimming with ghost chemistry, fearless and unspeakably cruel. Their leader is a Dread Exorcist. And they are performing a Monstrous Exorcism."

"Here? Now?"

"Of course! It's Friday the twenty-second."

"Ah. Thought that might be significant . . ."

"Friday the twenty-second is Exorcist's Day. They give each other cards and flowers, but they also do their most evil stuff. In fact, it was one thousand Fridays ago today, on a twenty-second, that the Dread Exorcist first made war on the school."

"How come I don't know about this?"

"It's not discussed. This was long before most of us died, and the few who were around back then won't talk about it. Shameful defeat and all."

"Drag."

"I only learned about the whole business a couple of days ago, from Dave, and even *he* didn't know anything about it until recently. Been doing research. Amazing guy, that Dave."

"No kidding. Where does he find this stuff out?"

"Stumbled across a library between the wall on the third floor. Whole section devoted to the secret history of the school."

"Now there's a place I wanna hang out."

Milrose could now see that the dim light in the corridor issued from tiny windows set into steel doors on either side. These doors looked as if they hadn't been opened in decades; some were even overgrown with moss. What behind them could possibly be producing light? Were they libraries? Archives? Showers?

"A thousand Fridays ago, according to lore, the

school engaged the services of this Vile Being. Quiet or he'll hear you. Seems they'd been trying to rid the school of ghosts for some time."

"What's all this anti-ghost sentiment? It's weird."

"Has to do with the school image. They're terrified that ghosts will make their way into the newspapers . . . or worse, into the official brochures. Bad for school rankings."

"Ah."

"So, they'd done their best, but the dead were fighting back. And the ghosts were winning. Man, I wish I could have seen it—according to Dave, they were doing some serious hardcore haunting: pencils screaming, textbooks moaning, blood dripping from the blackboards. Teachers were quitting by the boatload. The school *nurse* resigned!"

"Wow."

"And so the staff hired an exorcist. A very good one. The best. He was expensive, but they received a grant from the city."

"And this guy's here, now? In the basement?"

"Shh. We're getting close. He is wise amongst the wicked . . . very very strong. Managed to completely scour the first floor in time for an early lunch: dispatched the ghosts, one by one, and there were many. The goal, though—the reason he was hired— was to put a spell on the entire school. Render the whole building ghost-free for all time."

"Didn't pull that off, did he."

"No. There were a couple of pretty serious ghost chemists on the second floor, back in the day. Not trivial dudes. And they smote him with a counter-spell. He smote back. There was some mad smiting going on."

"Excellent."

"Finally, the dead guys succeeded in thwarting the Vile Being's most ambitious spell. They contained it: bound it up in thick chains of ghost chemistry, and the curse was restricted to the first floor. He man-aged to make that floor inhospitable to ghosts, very unpleasant if you're not alive, dead to the dead, but the chemists succeeded in rescuing the other floors from that fate."

A tiny dull light now floated in the distance, in the centre of the corridor.

"Man, who are these ghost chemists? I'd love to meet them."

"They're gone. The Exorcist . . . liquidated them."

"How do you liquidate a *ghost*? I mean, they're already dead."

"Horrible business. Don't want to go into it. But let's just say there are worse things than death. And the Dread Exorcist, in a final vicious blast, wasted the chemists who had thwarted his precious spell. As I say, this isn't discussed. It's a subject too terrify-ing even for most terrifying ghosts."

The corridor had at last come to an end: it was blocked by a steel door with a peephole set into it, through which the bleak light shone.

"Silence!" said Harry, although he was the only one making noise. "It is being accomplished here, behind this door!"

"He's *there*?"

"Yes! Dave figured out that it would be here, between the wall of the basement, that this walking terror would gather his minions. He is here, even now, doing unspeakable things. The unholy Archibald Loosten!"

"What?" said Milrose, in amused disbelief. "*Loosten*? The guidance counsellor?"

"He is more than a guidance counsellor," said Harry in a trembling whisper. "He is an exorcist. He is *the* exorcist. According to Dave, he is considered, in fact, the Mother of All Exorcists."

"How about that," said Milrose Munce. "Loosten. Who knew."

Harry approached the window and put his eye to the oculus.

"Archibald Loosten," mused Milrose. "Come on. How could this be? I mean, he wears a polyester suit."

"It is a disguise. And look at him now: revealed!"

Harry stood back, and Milrose, apprehensive, peered through the peephole. There, standing in a room on the other side, was Archibald Loosten, wearing a polyester suit, with a matching tie.

"Behold him," said Harry, "in his long flowing robes of satanic black, and breastplate of iron."

"Sure, Harry."

The guidance counsellor was addressing a small staff meeting.

"And lo," said Harry, "those are his minions. Mort Natoor, the assistant principal. Mrs. Ganneril, the dreaded secretary. Jimmy Mordred, the geography teacher. And on his way"—Harry shuddered—"is the janitor."

"The *janitor*? You mean old Fossilstiff is a turncoat? I *like* that guy."

"He is evil incarnate."

"Oh."

Milrose, although he was increasingly fond of Harry, was having a difficult time granting his observations much weight. Sure looked like a sad bunch of educators to him.

Archibald Loosten suddenly raised his open hand, however, and began an incantation; his voice was so loud in the corridor that the steel door might have been no more than a paper screen. And—was this possible?—his polyester suit shimmered and turned black, and grew long and billowy, and his matching tie widened into a spiked iron breastplate.

"Gosh," said Milrose.

Yes, things looked quite different now. Ganneril's hands dripped blood. Mort Natoor bore a fiery globe. Jimmy Mordred threw back his head and howled like a banshee.

Milrose did not recognize the language of Loosten's incantation. It was not the same as the one he had been memorizing; it sounded somehow uglier. He noted that Loosten's words were becoming visible, much as Dave's had, and were flying every which way. The most sinister ones seemed to be making their way through the ceiling.

"What is he *doing*?"

"Yeah, well. That's the concern. According to Dave, now would be the perfect opportunity—since a thousand Fridays have passed—for the Exorcist to make another go at that ambitious school-wide curse. After a thousand weeks, counterspells get kind of flimsy, and Magister Loosten probably figures he can finish the business this time. The local ghost chemists aren't quite as potent as they used to be."

"Hey, Dave's pretty fine," said Milrose indignantly.

"Yeah, and you're getting good, but many techniques have been lost. Loosten's clearly feeling bold. And . . . I don't want to think about what will happen to the dead if he succeeds."

"He won't. We won't let him!"

"It's crucial. It's been bad enough, the last thousand weeks, what with being confined to three" floors. And we've been cut off from the world of the living. Whenever we make friends with a live student, they . . . disappear."

"Aha!" said Milrose, about to venture a hypothesis. But just then Loosten gestured with high drama, and a door on the far side of the room flew open. There, glowering, stood Fossilstiff the janitor. Milrose had never noticed the janitor's horns before.

"Evidently," said Harry, "there used to be pretty good relations between the living and the dead. But Dave has this theory: whenever they notice that a student can see us, they send 'em off to Professional Help."

"Yerp. As always, the genius gets it right. Dave had us do some research, and yeah, good theory. He nailed it."

"And the only one who's ever returned from Professional Help is Sledge. Indestructible, I guess."

Milrose noted, nervously, that Loosten's incantation was growing in volume, and the flying words were growing claws, teeth, and the occasional moustache. He tried to remain casual. "But surely this works out nicely. I mean, once your friends are, uh, cured, doesn't that mean they sort of . . . well, join your ranks? I mean, you still get to hang out."

"Oh no. They don't die."

"Phew."

"It's worse."

"Oh."

"They get . . . removed. Erased. Annihilated. Same as what happened to those ghost chemists."

"Uh . . ."

"We don't talk about this."

"Excuse me, but, according to our calculations, Arabella and I are scheduled for a cure on Monday."

Harry had pulled Milrose from the door and was now peering through the peephole himself. He remained silent for a long time. "We must not fail."

"Right. Okay. Let's not."

"The time has come. Magister Loosten's in full swing. Here's the plan . . ."

Milrose, who was not accustomed to responsibility of any sort, forced himself to concentrate. This was his moment. All of that study—whole hours of it— would come to naught if he were to falter now. He closed his eyes and began a complex incantation.

It was nerve-racking to incant within earshot of Archibald Loosten, who was clearly a virtuoso, but Milrose found his voice growing firm as the words proceeded in the proper order from his lips. Yes, he *knew* this stuff. He flattened himself against the wall beside the door, to remain unseen. As his words grew in volume, the door between him and the evil gathering grew increasingly transparent. Magister Loosten looked about wildly as he heard the rival incantation—and Milrose brought it to a magnificent, incoherent conclusion.

The explosion was prodigious.

Harry, who had flattened himself against the ceiling above Milrose, whispered: "Yow!"

The incantation had been an exquisite success. The door was in shards. Loosten and his dread horde stared through it, aghast, and what they stared at was in fact ghastly. For barrelling down the corridor, with a truly unpleasant look in his eyes, was murderous Sledge.

"There's our man," whispered Harry from the ceiling. "Sledge. Terror of the Gridiron. Scourge of the Shower. Catastrophe of the Clubhouse."

Arabella had done her task well (a task she had long dreamed of). And now, from somewhere deep in the throat of Indomitable Sledge, came the choked words: "Professional Help."

Milrose prayed that Sledge would not deviate in his barrelling to note a small, sarcastic boy flattened against the wall.

"Professional Help," grunted Great Sledge as he made his murderous way, hands held out before him in an attitude of strangulation, towards Magister Loosten.

"Excuse me, Sledge," said Magister Loosten, but Sledge would not be stopped. "My dear Sledge, are you trying to provoke a detention?" But Sledge would not be slowed. "Um," Magister Loosten said, then spun in cowardice and squeezed past horned Fossilstiff through the door in the far wall. His robes became polyester and beige as he ran, and Sledge pursued with homicidal fury.

Heroic Sledge swatted Mort Natoor aside as if the assistant principal were a mere dung beetle. His pace would not waver, although Mrs. Ganneril clung to one of his huge legs and both Mordred and Fossilstiff to the other. For he was driven by vengeance.

"Sledge has never forgotten," whispered Harry, "that it was Magister Loosten who sentenced him to the Dungeons of Professional Help. Works in our favour, doesn't it."

The guidance counsellor disappeared down the corridor, and Sledge barrelled bellowing in his wake.

"Now's my chance," said Harry. "Wish me luck. And get back to the Den before the floor deplodes."

"Good luck," said Milrose. For Harry had determined that now, having engineered this general pandemonium amongst the forces of evil, it would be possible for a ghost—the first ghost in a thousand Fridays—to set foot on the first floor.

CHAPTER

NINE

IT HAD BEEN ALMOST THREE DAYS SINCE THE BAT-
TLE IN THE BASEMENT. ARABELLA AND MILROSE
PERCHED ON THE TOPMOST BUNK, CONFUSED AND
WORRIED. MILROSE HAD NOT WITNESSED ANY-
THING AFTER THE ESCAPE OF ARCHIBALD
LOOSTEN—HIS EXPLOSION WAS INDEED ABOUT
TO UNHAPPEN, AND HE HAD RUSHED BACK TO
CLIMB THE STEPLADDER WITH ARABELLA.

They'd heard no word from Harry. Had he managed to invade the first floor? (He had not intended
much of an invasion: simply to race up the stairs to
the second floor, with perhaps a couple of dead athletes. But merely passing through the first floor was,
of course, a giant leap for ghostkind.)

Friday afternoon was ominously silent. All day
Saturday they heard nothing. And now Sunday was

drawing to a close. On Monday, in a few short hours, they were destined to be cured.

"I don't get it," said Milrose. "The plan wasn't *that* complex—all he had to do was get to the second floor. Then it's easy. 'A coalition of the willing,' he called it—bring together dead guys from all three floors for a coordinated assault. I mean, surely he could get *some* of the ghosts to help out."

"I can't imagine my friends on the second floor would abandon us."

"I can." Milrose was busy imagining just that. "But the third floor's reliable—they're serious people—and Dave's the guy who set all this in motion, right? And even if my friends somehow . . . declined, where's Harry and his rotting jocks?"

As if in response to this, a familiar irritating voice descended from above.

"Munce? Munce, you there?" Harry's voice came through the ceiling like a keyhole saw.

"Boy, are we glad to hear you!" said Milrose.

The dead jockey luxuriated in these rare words.

"You made it, Harry! How are things on the second floor?"

"Second floor. Yeah. Wow, these guys are bad poets."

"No kidding. You have, uh, good news, right? You got past the ghost-free place . . . so you must have forces, like, arrayed?"

"Harold, why don't you come down here and join us."

"Um, I've kind of had my fill of the first floor."

"Come on, guy. This isn't the ordinary first floor. It's the *Den of Professional Help*! Whole different ball o' wax."

"Yeah, well, from what I've gathered it's even worse."

The worn soles of riding boots nevertheless appeared in the ceiling, and Harry began to descend, inch by inch, until his U-impressed head at last popped out, graced with a nervous expression.

Milrose Munce—who had never really warmed to any basement dweller before—threw his arms around the stunted ghost in a genuine embrace. Harry—who for his part had never considered himself all that embraceable—was taken aback, simultaneously flattered and appalled. This, however, served to blunt the recognition that he was now occupying the terrible first floor.

"Good to see you semi-intact, Harry. Welcome to our humble, like, abode," said Milrose.

"Er. Yeah. Cool place," said Harry without tremendous conviction.

"Lovely to see you again, Harold. I'm so happy you survived. Or whatever it is that ghosts do."

"Sure. Thanks."

"So, what was it like?"

"Like running up a flight of stairs, actually."

"Ah."

"Only infinitely more horrible."

"Yes."

"In fact, more like wading through a swamp with scorpions nibbling at your heels."

"I'm quite sure scorpions don't nibble, Harold."

"Okay, but you get the idea. Anyway, we made it. And now we're gonna get down to business and win this thing." He set what was left of his jaw. "We can't just phone this one in. We're aiming for *magnificence* here." Hurled Harry was beginning to take on the air of a tiny commander—a sort of crushed Napoleon— and his annoying voice was surprisingly effective in this role. "Munce? Chick? I'm talking *memorable*. We do this right, and years from now they'll be telling and retelling our story: in the teachers' lounge, at morning assemblies, in the great showers of post-game athletics. This is it, friends. Vengeance! With a capital V! Honour! With a capital O!"

"Harry, you're getting weirdly impressive."

"You only get one chance on the fields of glory," said Harry. "Okay, well, a couple, but I seriously messed up on the racetrack." This memory subdued him for a moment.

"Ancient history."

"Right. Right. And this time . . . this time I'm not gonna go it alone. This time I've got a *team*."

"Excellent! That's what I wanted to hear. You, uh, got our special poet on board?"

"Sure do. Had to rough him up a bit."

"Of course."

"This Poisoned character. Any way of shutting his yap?"

"Can't be done, I'm afraid. I've been trying for ages."

"He read a three-hundred-page poem at me. No stopping him. It was godawful."

"Ah. *The Flavour of Indigestion?*"

"That's the one!"

"He's been working hard. Used to be only seventy pages or so."

"It *sucks*."

"Well, yes. So, he's going to help out?"

"Unfortunately. Uh, Munce? What exactly do you need a poet for?"

"Secret weapon of mass destruction, Harry. I'll let you in on the strategy when it's time. But make sure he brings that manuscript. So, where do we stand now, victory-wise?"

"I like to think we stand on the razor's edge, staring into the abyss."

"Er, that's good, right?"

"If you like that kind of thing. Question of attitude. We won that battle in the basement, far as I can tell, pretty decisively. But Loosten's incantation managed to do a fair bit of damage. You can feel it on the second floor: that scorpion/swamp feeling. He's managed to make the rest of the school pretty hairy for us dead guys. And it's one of those spells that keeps on working once it's been spoken—gets worse by the hour."

"Can't you, maybe, smite it or something? Counterspell?"

"Who knows. Not my territory, that. I'm just working on getting you out of here before you get whacked."

"I do wish you wouldn't use that word, Harold."

"Cured. Whatever."

"Right. Okay. So, we've got our team. Now what?"

"Not a lot. Wait for us. But here's the thing. There's gonna be a lot of pressure on you to be, uh, cured before we get a chance to intervene. Just so you know."

"Great."

"And you can't do that. It's important. You can't get whacked until we win this thing. Then you can feel free to get whacked all you want."

"Noted."

"That's all."

"Any, like, pointers? How to, you know, not get whacked?"

Arabella winced with great sensitivity.

"Sorry, can't help. Anyway, I have to be off—gotta rally the troops. Dunno when precisely we're going to be able to come to your aid, but look for us on the morrow."

"On the morrow? Where you channelling this sick stuff from, Harry?"

"He's a poet," said Arabella. "It is being breathed into him from the mysterious place."

"Right," said Harry, not pleased. "Catch you."

And with that he floated up through the ceiling.

Harry's martial confidence had lifted their spirits. Hope infused terror. The two spoke in excited tones for hours, and then Arabella decided that she could no longer sustain excitement (which was trying for her at the best of times).

"I am too tired to think about this anymore," said Arabella. "Good night, Milrose."

"Good night, fair and winsome nay wholesome maiden," said Milrose, meaning to say "goodnight, Arabella." (Words were once again beyond his immediate control.)

Arabella gave him an odd, but perhaps apprecia-tive, look, and Milrose met this with misty, ridiculous eyes.

Monday arrived, fully accursed and ominous. It took a while before revealing its true nature, but yes: this looked to be a day that would move them inexorably in the direction of mutually inflicted death. Or worse.

The first part of the morning was deceptively innocuous: a harmless—if mindless—exercise designed to nudge Milrose and Arabella in the direction of normalcy. They were made to flip through magazines, and to discuss the celebrities encountered there with loud enthusiasm. Both felt they were pulling this off quite well.

"Isn't that Brad fellow *rad?*" said Arabella, doing her very best impression of everybody she loathed.

Unfortunately, this exercise had simply been a warm-up, Massimo announced, for the one they were now to engage in—one that would go a long way towards improving their relations with each other and the world. Today, in order to make great leaps towards normalcy, they would do a particularly intensive exercise in trust.

"One moment," he said, "while I retrieve the mace. Oh, and here are your blindfolds."

All of Arabella's irrational self-possession drained away. She had been doing such a fine job of banishing that medieval device from her mind. As Massimo fiddled with the mace closet, Arabella stared with terror at Milrose. She produced two whole tears, one from each eye, then bowed her head so that they raced each other down the sides of her nose to join pendulously at the tip. "I'm sorry, Milrose," she whispered. The conjoined tear quivered, and then disengaged from her lovely nose to fall horribly upon the floor.

Milrose, who had never encountered anything like this degree of emotion in his den mate, came very close to weeping himself—and not in his traditional almost-but-not-really-sincere manner.

They stared at each other, with tenderness and dread. And then the ceiling opened above them.

Unseen by any of the three, who had no particular reason to be looking up, the door in the ceiling swung downward, and as Massimo turned back towards the couple, proudly bearing the mace, Hurled Harry descended heroically.

Milrose Munce saw him first. Arabella turned to see what had inspired Milrose with sudden glee, and Hurled Harry opened his arms, palms upwards, to indicate: "Fear not, fair chick, I am here."

Massimo Natica, of course, saw nothing. For he had not been gifted with the ability to see the glorious dead.

In the wake of Hurled Harry, as if rappelling on invisible ropes, came the rest of the rotting SWAT team. Ghoul after ghoul. First in the vanguard was Third Degree Thor, a bruising Sledge wannabe who had long ago caught fire when he collided with a cheerleader twirling a fiery baton. Next came Desiccated Douglas, who had become lost during an orienteering championship in the desert. Third was Stuck Stu, master of self-combustion. And fourth, much to the excitement of Milrose Munce, was that master of general combustion, that wizard in the matter of all things that could be made to fly into molten pieces: Deeply Damaged Dave. Dave winked at Milrose, and flexed a muscle.

Wafting down last, clearly terrified, was Poisoned Percy, clutching a manuscript.

Massimo Natica glanced at his watch. "Ah," he said, placing the mace on the comfy sofa, "our exercise in trust will have to wait. It is time for lunch!"

Arabella sat gracefully on a chair, successfully preventing herself from fainting with relief.

Massimo removed the key from his pocket and unlocked the alarmingly modern lock, which this time made the unambiguous sound of sperm whales being slaughtered. He was passed the habitual tray by the beast with beastly arms. He closed and locked the door.

As Massimo carried the tray over to his famished Helpees, he was tailed by Stuck Stu, who had been an amateur thief before devoting himself to science. Stu quickly and deftly removed the chillingly modern key from the pocket of that swish suit.

As always, they sat in a little circle on the floor and helped themselves to lunch. The little circle was, however, somewhat larger today. The three athletes, two science victims, and token poet gathered around as well, in various inspired positions.

Desiccated Douglas, a parched ghoul who looked much like an unwound mummy, laid himself out next to Massimo as if posing for a fashion magazine. Douglas sucked his cheeks in, just as he'd seen male models do in order to make themselves more attractive. Now, almost *anything* would have made Douglas more attractive, in that he could hardly get much worse, but this sucking in of cheeks was in fact the one thing capable of making Douglas even more repulsive. Considerably more repulsive. His skin had dried and tightened against his skull—not all that fetching at the best of times—and when he sucked in what was left of his cheeks, this dried skin stretched transparent, revealing all sorts of things you really didn't want to see.

"Peel me another grape," whispered Desiccated Douglas.

"I beg your pardon?" said Massimo to Milrose.

"I didn't say anything," said Milrose, smiling.

"I thought you said pass the grapes. Or something."

"There are no grapes, Massimo."

"Well, yes." Massimo frowned and shrugged. He resumed his lunch.

Stuck Stu sat in a lotus position beside Massimo and mocked his every gesture. When Massimo reached for a sandwich, Stu reached for the same sandwich, but then drew his hand away in disgust, as if the sandwich were mouldy. It was difficult to imagine anything causing Stu disgust, given the great volume of disgust his presence inspired in the world. Despite having pulled himself together considerably in death, pieces of him were still missing. And lots of pieces of him—bones, for instance—were a bit too prominent.

He burped, loudly. Massimo looked at Milrose severely. "That's not like you, Milrose."

"What's not like me?"

"To . . . not say excuse me."

"Um, excuse me? Why would I say excuse me?"

"For . . . burping."

"I beg your pardon?"

"That's better."

"I mean, I beg your pardon, but I didn't burp, Massimo."

Massimo frowned. He resumed his lunch. Then he looked up at Milrose through suspicious eyes. Then he resumed his lunch.

Third Degree Thor, who was so revolting that it would not be in good taste to describe him here, sat between Milrose and Arabella and stared directly into Massimo Natica's eyes with his own (which had melted, unfortunately, but could still manage an approximation of a stare). He licked his lips in an exaggerated manner whenever Massimo chewed.

"Mmmm," said Third Degree Thor.

"Enjoying your sandwich, are you, Milrose?"

"Not particularly. Why do you ask?"

"Were you being sarcastic, then?"

"I wasn't being anything, Massimo."

"But . . ." Massimo shook his head, as if attempting to dislodge something from his ear.

Hurled Harry cleared his throat. Massimo glanced quickly at Arabella. Poisoned Percy sneezed. Massimo glanced quickly at Milrose Munce. All very normal, said his worried expression: all very normal for people to clear their throats and sneeze. Except that these clearings and sneezings did not emit, precisely, from the place they ought to—which is to say the throat of Arabella and the nose of Milrose Munce.

Massimo jerked a shoulder, involuntarily, as if a heavy fly had landed upon it.

Third Degree Thor, who had an excess of athletic energy at all times, was too bored to remain seated for long in this congenial circle. He tiptoed dramatically over to the antique cattle prod. Hypermasculine Thor was not one to tiptoe, and it did not suit his physique at all. He opened the glass cabinet, carefully and quietly, and removed the prod, then tiptoed back to stand behind Massimo Natica. To the great amusement of all, he held the prod just above and behind Massimo, and mimed the activity of sending great jolts of electricity into that immaculate head. As Thor pretended to zap Massimo, he pulled his own hair up, to make it look as if it were standing on end, while simultaneously assuming an expression—insofar as a charred head can express—of "Help, I'm being electrocuted!"

Massimo Natica, sensing that something was behind him, turned to look. Luckily, Thor had the hairtrigger impulses of a crack jock, and he quickly moved the cattle prod so that it remained behind Massimo's magnificent head.

What Massimo did see was that the glass case in which the prod was usually kept was open and empty. He looked piercingly at Milrose Munce. "Where is the cattle prod?"

"I'm not sure. Where did you leave it?"

"I did not take it out."

"Well then, it must be in the case."

"Does it look as if it's in the case?"

"Yes."

Massimo swivelled his head sharply. And there was the antique prod, lying where it was supposed to lie. Thor had not managed to close the glass door, however.

Massimo Natica turned back to Milrose and pointed an irate finger. "The case is open!"

"That's not the case."

"What do you mean? That *is* the case. It's where the cattle prod's *always* kept!"

"No, I mean that's not the case. That the case, in this case, is open."

Massimo did not turn to look back at the prod. No, he knew very well what he would see, as his hallucinations were becoming predictable. He closed his eyes tightly and shook his head, as if attempting to dislodge a small tumour from his brain. And then, with a look of sad resignation, he turned very slowly to look at the case, which was of course now closed.

Third Degree Thor was standing beside the glass cabinet, triumphantly, his hands spread before him as if he were an Italian chef exalting the veal Milanese: "Look at my exceptional performance!"

For once, Milrose Munce was not at all annoyed by Thor's tendency to brag. He snorted.

"Why are you snorting?"

"Um . . ."

"You *did* snort! I heard it! It was *you*, snorting!"

"Why yes it was, Massimo."

This silenced the Professional Helper completely. The last thing he expected was that the snort would be acknowledged by Milrose Munce.

"So, it was . . . your snort."

"Precisely as you said. You called it perfectly."

"Oh." He paused. "You're sure now?"

"As sure as the prod in your case."

"That's not an expression!"

"Pardon me. I was being inventive. An old family trait, in fact, invention. My great-great-grandfather patented a device for exploding pimples. Very economical, as it required only a pinch of gunpowder . . ."

Massimo Natica was so confused that he did not think to insist upon an answer to the initial question: namely, *why* this snort.

For the next few minutes, the ghostly army did nothing but laze about. They gave Massimo time to calm himself, and to dismiss the recent peculiarities as something he had perhaps imagined. The mind is good at this, when faced with what it very much does not wish to believe.

Hurled Harry was proving a freakishly talented tactician. For this was precisely the thing to do: allow Massimo to regain his sanity, so that the next assault would again wrench him but good. It's far less wrenching to go from insane to slightly more insane. No, Harry had it all figured out: he wanted Massimo Natica's brain to swing like a pendulum—from reality to nightmare and back again—with him, Harry, holding the end of the rope.

Milrose was truly impressed. This fit well with his own stroke of tactical genius, which he welcomed the opportunity to reveal to Hurled Harry, their commander-in-chief. For Poisoned Percy, nervously clutching his manuscript and not yet joining in the fun, would be the cherry on top of the cake, the froth on the cappuccino, and the straw to break the camel's back.

Much remained to be resolved. Although Harry had been briefed regarding the exercises in trust and bodily destruction, none were sure what precise exercise Massimo had in store for this afternoon.

"This afternoon," said Massimo, "we shall leave the blindfolds off."

This would have been a relief, except that it wasn't. In some ways it was better *not* to see the doom that was rushing down upon you like a blind and leprous bull.

"Now, you are to stand face to face."

Milrose and Arabella, despite themselves, were soon standing face to face. Unfortunately, the ghouls had also paired up: Dave and Douglas, Stu and Harry, Thor and—although Thor's expression suggested he was clearly not happy with his draw— Poisoned Percy.

Milrose Munce's hopes recoiled in horror. These dead students had no more ability to withstand the concentrated will of Massimo Natica than did he or Arabella. Harry and his soldiers were also going to find themselves perpetrating exercises in trust. This scenario tested even the highly elastic imagination of Milrose Munce. This was going to prove, at the very least, weird.

"Right. Now, you are to place your index fingers

upon the closed eyelids of your partner. Good. And with subtle pressure . . ."

But the dreaded exercise was never announced. For a small, pretentious voice began to recite:

> *"The stomach is the place of ill-content.*
> *For in the fluids that are gathered there*
> *You find the decomposing stomach sludge . . ."*

"Where is that ridiculous voice coming from?" asked Massimo Natica, sounding both indignant and fearful.

> *"And in that sludge will barely make a dent*
> *The kidney's fetid arrows, sleek with hair . . ."*

"And who wrote that vile poem?"

Milrose Munce, who would never have imagined himself actually *joyful* to hear Poisoned Percy recite from *The Flavour of Indigestion*, was not simply joyed but overjoyed. This in fact was the secret weapon he had in mind: when all else failed, he intended to wheel out the dreadful poet, for nothing is a blow to the sanity like truly execrable verse. And doubly terrifying is execrable verse emerging, apparently, from nowhere. For Massimo Natica had never seen a ghost, and could not see any now—Percy the Poseur had simply made it possible for Massimo to *hear* him.

The common ability to make oneself heard, while invisible, is useful to a ghost—when howling in a darkened house, for instance. Or when proudly declaiming ambitious poetry from beyond the grave.

"And though between the organs you do trudge . . ."

Yes, Poisoned Percy, though utterly without taste, was gifted with a *large* and tasteless imagination, and it is this that permitted him to think his way out of the spell woven by Massimo Natica. For in the mind of Poisoned Percy, nothing was more powerful than his own poetry. And he knew that reciting that poetry would break whatever chain was wrapped around his pretentious soul.

It was remarkably effective. Massimo pressed his hands to his ears and looked as if he might throw up. This released the spell upon the finger-to-eyelid couples, and they immediately drew apart. Those ghosts who did not in fact have eyelids were relieved to have the fingers removed from what was left of their eyeballs.

Percival, always pleased to have an audience, rose to new heights of abysmal depth. His voice grew in confidence and volume.

"And flabby though your ventricle is bent
Your peach will ne'er be sweet meat to her pear . . ."

"What is this *garbage?*" howled Massimo.

Everyone else in the room, although fully in agreement with that critical assessment, was truly enjoying the poem.

Freed, now, to continue their assault upon the wits of Massimo Natica, they flew into action.

"No, never will zucchinis match that food
Which of the gods we eat and yet are greased . . ."

Harry met the glittering eye of Milrose Munce and nodded with soldierly appreciation. Yes, said Harry's nod, I now recognize your peculiar genius. True, it was more peculiar than genius, yet who but Milrose Munce—perfected in sarcasm and tutored in pretense by the very best—could possibly imagine the necessity of bringing this puissant, ineluctable force to the battlefield: Rancid Poetry.

TEN

SO POTENT WAS PERCY THAT HE COULD EASILY HAVE DOWNED THE PROFESSIONAL HELPER ON HIS OWN. HURLED HARRY, HOWEVER, HAD ORCHESTRATED A MAGNIFICENT PLAN, AND IT SEEMED UNFAIR NOT TO ALLOW HIS FOOT SOL-DIERS TO FOLLOW THROUGH.

Thor whispered something into Arabella's ear. She happily obliged, removing her ballet slippers and passing them to the flambéed star of the grid-iron. Massimo did not see this transaction, but he was soon very much aware of Arabella's footgear. For Third Degree Thor had put the slippers on his hands, with Arabella helping to fasten the silken straps around his wrists. And Massimo was about to experience a ballet unlike anything ever choreo-graphed by man.

As the rest of the brave soldiers set about preparing to play their part, Thor began to dance.

To be more precise: Thor's hands began to dance. He got down on all fours, and made his hands walk, with light and easy steps, towards Massimo Natica. Massimo, when he finally noticed this, of course saw nothing more than a pair of ballet slippers, sans ballerina, tippy-toeing his way.

He drew back in horror. And, forgetting himself, let his hands fall from his ears.

"And rotting gourds will take the place of meat . . ."

The slippers whirled and tapped and hovered in mid-air. And stood and jumped and slapped Massimo Natica playfully across the face.

Thor was enjoying this act. For at the heart of every football player resides a ballerina. He himself was now unnecessarily on his tiptoes, pirouetting and assuming what he imagined were professional ballet poses. While occasionally deigning to chuck Massimo playfully beneath the chin.

"And though we munch and belch and bleat
and brood . . ."

Were Massimo concentrating elsewhere but upon the invisible ballerina that was tormenting him, he might have cause for alarm. Yes, he already had some cause for alarm, but this would have been cause for *alarm*. For the cattle prod was rising out of its case, as if on invisible wings.

Stuck Stu hovered close to the ceiling, bearing this electrical device. He examined it with a frown. How do you start up an antique cattle prod? Luckily, Stu had been a budding engineer back in the carefree days when he was healthy and whole, and he was soon able to figure out the mechanism. It was quite simple, really: there was a switch.

Stu made a dramatic show of throwing the switch, and the cattle prod hummed to life.

What proved particularly useful, and unexpected, was the prod's high-pitched whine, which sounded very much like a mosquito. It became immediately clear to Stuck Stu that he need not actually *assault* Massimo with the prod; he need not *electrocute* him; it might prove even more amusing to simply *annoy* him.

And so great Stu descended with the prod held in front of him, and flew around the Professional Helper's head. This was no ordinary irritation: Massimo soon realized that the noise was being produced not by anything so merely annoying as a mosquito, but by a capricious, floating cattle prod—an entirely different order of annoyance.

The ballet slipper tickled his ear.

"And though the foul lung flesh is our feast
And cells of dribbling liver suck that teat . . ."

Harry stood in the middle of the room, like an orchestra conductor, and flamboyantly gestured to Stu that now, indeed, was the time to indicate to Massimo that there was *no way out.*

This was impeccably timed. Massimo had just begun to frantically search his pockets, seeking his appallingly modern key.

The key was, in fact, hovering in front of his nose. Massimo snatched at it in desperation, but it was now hanging playfully over his head. He slapped at it, hoping to trap it between his hand and his scalp, but he only succeeded in hitting himself rather hard, as the key fluttered off to dangle beside his left ear.

"Another pink and gaseous song will squat . . ."

Milrose Munce and Arabella briefly wondered what further part they were to play in this theatrical extravaganza. But it was soon obvious to them that anything this entertaining would require an audience. And so they sat side by side on the comfy sofa and watched with delight the unravelling of Massimo Natica's mind.

"It shall arise from nodules yet unpricked . . ."

Desiccated Douglas, who had been waiting impatiently in the wings, was now set into motion by maestro Harold. Douglas had a subtle role, involving a very unsubtle object. He placed the mace on the floor in front of him and began to move it slowly towards Massimo Natica. It was a very un-mace-like motion. The weapon slithered. It rolled. It meandered. And yet it approached.

This was the most brutal assault yet (apart from the poetry, of course, with which nothing could remotely compete), for the mace, which would have been pretty frightening were it swinging properly, was utterly terrifying because it was not. What is it going to *do?* wondered Massimo in desperation. Why is it *slithering?*

And yet all the mace really did was slither. It snaked and circled about his feet; it withdrew, coyly, then made another surreal pass.

"It shall excuse the glandular guitar . . ."

Massimo Natica ducked and wove, fear alternating with madness in his eyes, as the cattle prod whined and soared, the key dangled and darted, the slippers slipped, and the mace meandered, slithersome.

Hurled Harry stood gesticulating majestically: he was indeed conducting all of this as if it were a symphony.

At one point these various activities came together in such a powerfully dramatic fashion that Milrose Munce and Arabella were moved to a spontaneous standing ovation.

And to punctuate that glorious crescendo, Desiccated Douglas swung the great mace, shattering the almost invulnerable window set high into the steel door.

"Act Two," announced Harry in the silence that followed.

Whatever Hurled Harry had planned for his second act was immediately upstaged by a drama so utterly convincing that you could never imagine such a thing being scripted or rehearsed. Or tolerated by a responsible stage manager.

The repulsively modern lock suddenly whirred and clicked—accompanied by the sound of leprechauns gagging—and flew open to admit the almost airborne person of Archibald Loosten.

"Aiee!" cried the poor guidance counsellor as he dove behind a comfy chair.

"Professional Help," growled Sledge as he barrelled into the room in pursuit. Barrelling equally ferociously, since Sledge had him in a headlock, was the brute who had all this time been delivering their meals.

"Mr. Borborygmus!" said Milrose Munce with

genuine surprise. "I never before noticed what large and brutish arms you have."

The poor trapped teacher had no time to reply, as Sledge continued to barrel, marvellous in momentum, straight into the wall opposite the door. He probably would have broken (or re-broken) that appalling nose, had not the head of Borborygmus barrelled into the wall first.

The room crunched. Not just the wall—which did not in fact splinter—but the room itself crunched. And creaked. And groaned horribly, as it tipped, slowly but with ineluctable motion, until it settled on its side.

Nobody had ever seen a room roll over before. The wall was now the floor. The ceiling was now the wall. And—marvel of marvels—the door in the ceiling was now a perfectly placed exit.

"I have a headache," said Borborygmus, who had not been otherwise damaged.

"Professional Help," growled Sledge, and immediately continued in his barrelling, dragging unfortunate Mr. Borborygmus at great speed through the newly accessible door.

Nothing happened for a moment or so. What does one do when the room in which one has been standing is suddenly tipped on its side? Obviously, the first thing to do is pick yourself up from the brand-new floor, onto which you have been tipped along with all the room's furniture, knickknacks, and weaponry. Nobody was horribly hurt, but everyone was copiously confused.

And into the midst of this confusion wandered Cryogenic Kelvin, with a beaming smile on his cadaverous face.

"Milrose, old pal!" said Kelvin, pleased to see his friend alive and merely bruised. "So this is it, huh? The famed Den of Professional Help. Just came down to see what all the racket was. Place sure is a mess . . ."

Creeping slowly towards the door, trying hard not to be noticed, was half-mad Massimo Natica, whose hair was mussed and suit slightly wrinkled. "Massimo the Mediocre!" cried Kelvin, immediately recognizing the Professional Helper. Cryogenic Kelvin made himself fully visible, fully hideous and standing between the Helper and the doorway, just to make sure that Massimo would be dissuaded from exiting that way.

Hysterical with terror—and worse, insulted— Massimo scampered, still on all fours, into a complex mess formed by a group of thrown chairs. He disappeared like a lizard beneath a rock.

"You know this guy?" asked Milrose in wonder.

"Just by reputation. Seen his picture a few times. He was on a poster, you know."

"A what?"

"A poster. Circus poster! Famously bad act."

"Massimo Natica is a clown?"

"Well, he is a clown, but that was not his official position in the circus. The not-quite-famous Rotting Apple Circus."

Cryogenic Kelvin was clearly about to launch into an anecdote. Nobody was in the mood to stop him. In fact, nobody was in the mood to do much of anything. And so they listened.

"Yes, I have friends from the Rotting Apple. Briefly dated a dead contortionist, in fact. But I treated her bad, and she got a little bent out of shape."

Kelvin stopped, as always, to gather the response to his punchline. Milrose chuckled weakly.

"And she told me all about Massimo the Mediocre. Billed as the greatest hypnotist ever to swing a watch. Used to hypnotize the whole audience. Problem is, all he ever managed to do was put them half asleep. And so, no matter how good the rest of the show, the audience would just sit there yawning, bored to distraction. It took hours before they properly emerged from this hypnotic state, by which time they were usually at home telling their friends what an incredibly dull circus they had just witnessed. Didn't do much for the Rotting Apple's reputation."

"Hm," said Milrose. "His skills have improved."

"Well, yes. They were already getting better at the time of the disaster. He had progressed from being

Massimo the Massively Awful to Massimo the Merely Mediocre. He was to the point where he could now put a group of people fully to sleep. And this, my friends, was the problem."

"You don't have to tell this anecdote!" cried Massimo Natica from his hiding place between the chairs.

"Of course not," said Kelvin. "You never *have* to tell any particular anecdote, do you. You just do it, purely for the entertainment value."

"This is not entertaining!"

"Not for you, clearly. How about you, Milrose? You entertained?"

"Wildly," said Milrose. Which was not far from the truth.

"Me too," said Thor.

"Got me hooked," said Harry.

"I am enjoying this, yes," said Arabella.

"You might use a more luscious vocabulary," said Percy.

"Right, then," said Kelvin. "To continue. Oh, and shut up, Percy. Yes, Massimo had mastered the art of the collective snooze. Didn't matter who you were, or what you were doing—Massimo could send you straight to slumberville.

"The disaster occurred during a rehearsal. Everyone was practising their act for the big day ahead, when they were to open in front of their largest audience ever. They had never been more than a two-ring circus, and at last the Michelin Guide had granted them a third ring. It was the final rehearsal, and for this they never used safety nets or padding.

"The trapeze artists flung and the acrobats flipped. The clowns clowned. The lion tamer tamed. And Massimo rehearsed his routine."

Cryogenic Kelvin paused for effect. It was not a punchline, true, but it was equally deserving of a moment's dramatic silence, for clearly something very bad was about to happen. Kelvin made sure that everyone's breath was properly bated before he continued.

"Yes, Massimo the Newly Semi-Competent went through his tedious act, to be sure that he was in shape for the next day's show. And he was good. Best ever. Every single person in the tent fell asleep.

"The trapeze artists began to snore mid-air, and fell with great squashing noises to the floor below. The acrobats, who thought they could do triple flips in their sleep, in fact could not. Also breaking their necks were the contortionists—including my darling ex—since they were tied into the sort of knot in which you really aren't supposed to relax, much less fall into a hypnotic coma. The lion tamer fell asleep, but the lion itself did not, which was regrettable. Even the clowns, who were walking on their hands, sustained concussions, and died the next morning of brain fever while telling confused jokes.

"The ringleader, who alone survived, had no choice but to fire Massimo the Mediocre."

"He didn't fire me," piped up Massimo Natica. "He accepted my resignation."

"That's not how my girlfriend told the story. At any rate, fascinating to bump into you. Always wondered where they'd put a has-been hypnotist out to pasture."

"Well, this explains a lot," said Milrose Munce. "We kind of questioned why we were doing all the mindless and murderous things this fraud suggested."

"I am not a fraud," wheedled Massimo. "I am a Professional."

"Diploma?" asked Arabella, diplomatically.

"It's in my drawer," said Massimo Natica, with even less credibility than usual.

"I have searched your drawers," said Deeply Damaged Dave, who had been until now uninvolved in the general merriment, "and they are free of any form of accreditation."

Milrose was excited to see his mentor at last join in the ritual humiliation: he expected great things.

"And you," said Dave with great authority, pointing at a sofa, "are hereby stripped of your licence to cause misery."

Mr. Loosten's head slowly rose from behind the

sofa. He had the look of a cornered weasel: terrified, but cruelly determined. The flabby mouth opened, and an incomprehensible incantation began to emerge.

"Put a cork in it, Loosten," said Dave, who then suddenly launched into a fearful incantation of his own, also incomprehensible, but much more impressive than Loosten's diminished efforts. A giant cork appeared in the air, conjured up from nothing, and hovered in front of the Dread Exorcist's face. As Dave's incantation rose to a pitch of fearful incomprehensibility, the cork whirled and flew at the guidance counsellor, lodging solidly in his mouth and effectively bottling him up. His own incantation was reduced to a muffled grunt of distress.

Clearly, Dave had become staggeringly good at all sorts of ghost chemistry, some of it almost subtle.

With the evil guidance counsellor silenced, Dave began to incant in earnest. He produced a large notebook from a bag he was carrying, opened it, and began to read from it—or, rather, sing from it: a more tuneful brand of incomprehensible syllables.

"New counterspell!" Kelvin whispered into the ear of Milrose Munce. "And a really good one. Wow. He's exceeding himself."

Even the mortals could sense it: as Dave sang from his notes, the spell on the first floor was coming undone. A prodigious creaking filled the air.

Loosten worked his face and grunted, but whatever
spell he was desperately trying to conjure in
response was stopped short by the massive cork.
The creaking was punctuated by the occasional
crunch. It grew in volume. The crunches become
less occasional. As Dave's voice majestically crescen-
doed, both creak and crunch were for a moment
unbearably loud, and the entire room swam blindly
in a shared headache. And then it was over.

The ghosts cheered. Deeply Damaged Dave, his
chanting accomplished, closed his notebook and—
for an encore—casually made a comfy chair explode.

Led by Milrose, Arabella, and flower, the victors
departed the Den of Professional Help. First followed the warriors (scientific, athletic, and poetic);
then Cryogenic Kelvin, carrying the mace (which
would add a dash of spice to his next performance in
Biology); penultimately, at some distance, the red-
faced and disgraced Massimo the Mediocre; and
finally—dismissed and all but forgotten—a corked
and completely powerless Archibald Loosten.

The new exit from the Den opened, surprisingly,
into the hallway where you could never, at one time,
turn left. From this door, you turned right. Nobody
thought to look back when the procession had
finally made its way through that door and down
the hall, but if they had they would have noted that

this exit, so newly arrived in this world, had disappeared. No, you could no longer turn left, and never in the long future of the school was it possible to turn in that direction again.

In the weeks that followed, much was changed among both the living and the dead.

Massimo Natica disappeared, but word was that he had run away to find work in another circus—the Sleazy Peach Pit—considered by many the very worst circus in the world. Because his reputation preceded him like a foul wind, however, even this stumbling troupe had taken him only after he hypnotized them during the interview so that they awoke to an iron-clad contract.

Mr. and Mrs. Munce were of course mortified and riddled with parental guilt when they discovered the true nature of their son's Professional Help. They staged a noisy revolt at the next meeting of the Parent-Teacher Association, as a result of which the staff at the school was adjusted.

Mr. Fossilstiff was pushed into early retirement. Mr. Borborygmus, even though his intelligence had not been affected in the slightest by his encounter with the wall, now worked in the cafeteria. And Archibald Loosten was demoted to janitor.

Mrs. Ganneril, Mort Natoor, and Jimmy Mordred were subtly pressured to resign. They joined together as a team of Professional Consultants, and enjoyed modest success.

The old principal, who does not enter this story because he had absolutely no idea what was going on right beneath his ancient hairy nostrils, left to become president of the national school board.

This reorganization was handled with great efficiency by the new principal, whose nomination had in fact been suggested first by Milrose Munce and then pursued with ardour by his guilty parents. It was an inspired choice, and Caroline Corduroy thrived and blossomed in her new position.

The general presence of ghosts was no longer a secret to many in the school, although the staff and parents agreed that it was best to keep this information out of the brochures. Archibald Loosten, janitor, wept when he discovered how easy this was to accomplish—all of those wars and spells and counterspells had been entirely unnecessary.

The ex-exorcist was a pathetic creature now, but nobody could be entirely certain that he did not retain a few malevolent powers. And so the wise Ms. Corduroy hired a new teacher of home economics who was also a famed and feared white warlock. Archibald Loosten—even if he should have been mopping the hall—did not dare to set foot on the first floor when a home ec class was in progress.

Deeply Damaged Dave now spent all of his time

in the library between the wall of the third floor, composing what would become the classic reference text on the uses and abuses of ectoplasmic manipulation. Milrose benefited greatly from his research, and any one object in his vicinity was increasingly in danger of becoming, if only for a temporary stretch, multiple.

Despite what Milrose predicted, Bored Beulah and Arabella became fast friends. Beulah's diffidence complemented Arabella's pretense; together they were an impressively weird and unapproachable pair. They spent a great deal of time together on the first floor, which was now a cheerful place that rang with the voices of the decomposed.

Milrose Munce, too, had broadened his group of friends to include all sorts of new species and categories. He spent whole entertaining afternoons with Hurled Harry, whose voice had settled into the near bearable range now that he carried himself with Napoleonic authority. Harry was no longer used as a medicine ball, and he in fact outlawed this practice in the basement. Third Degree Thor proved to have a remarkable if blunt sense of humour, and Milrose found him almost worth the occasional conversation. Milrose was even taking pride in being chosen second-last for baseball teams, and had once risen to third-last (although he was never permitted to actually play).

The second floor was an increasingly congenial place. Milrose Munce found to his surprise that he enjoyed the company of poseurs—balladeers, new-media artists, and scrimshaw carvers—especially the few who had a nano-sliver of talent. Percy and Milrose were now on tolerable terms—and in his better moods Milrose would even call him Parsifal.

One sunny afternoon Milrose Munce was summoned to the principal's office. This was not a call he feared in the slightest. In fact, even if it portended punishment, Milrose relished the thought of such a visit. Sadly, punishment in general did not happen to him all that often anymore. Teachers were careful not to upset Mr. and Mrs. Munce, who had risen to positions of prominence in the Parent-Teacher Association. Milrose Munce's behaviour, though, had in no way improved—Professional Help had been, thankfully, useless. And having proven himself in battle had in no way gone to his head, or made him any more likely to enjoy Phys. Ed. It had, on the other hand, made him feel a much greater responsibility to experiment with and master every explosive material known to man.

"Come in, Milrose."

"Greetings, Fair Principal."

"Sit down, Milrose."

"What horribly wrong thing have I done now?"

asked Milrose Munce, as he lounged casually upon the chair in front of Ms. Corduroy's desk.

"I have here," said the principal, "the poem you wrote during your last detention."

Now that Caroline Corduroy helmed the school, epic poems had become the standard punishment during detention. This was a particular headache for members of the football team, although Ig had a knack for stringing together obscene limericks.

"Oh man," said Milrose. "Don't try to tell me there are *any* inappropriate sentences in that poem. That's a clean piece of poetry."

Milrose had initially made a habit, under the new detention regimen, of inserting highly unbefitting passages in the middle of his epics; they were rarely discovered, as few teachers had the fortitude to read juvenile epics all the way through. A couple of teachers, unfortunately, displayed rare stamina, and Milrose was mending his ways.

"That is what I wished to discuss with you. I am greatly disappointed. Severely disappointed."

"What? That I haven't given you cause to, I dunno, send me out for Professional Help?"

"We do not employ Professional Help anymore, Milrose. You of all people ought to be aware of this."

"Oh yeah. I like to think I had a small part to play, even, in that little area of institutional reform."

"Do not flatter yourself."

"Okay."

"Since that is what *I* must regretfully do."

"You? Flatter *me*?"

"Please relax. I fully expect never to have cause to do it again. However. Milrose, not only is this poem full of appropriate sentences—" Caroline Corduroy sighed, with great sadness, "but it's actually quite *good*."

Milrose was shocked. "I didn't *mean* it . . ."

"I know. And you will not be punished. Still, it is of scientific and medical interest that you have developed a poetic soul."

"Do they have treatment for this?"

"As far as I know it cannot be reversed."

"Darn." Milrose Munce had of course already been made aware of his soul drifting in this direction, but it was nice to have independent corroboration. "Hey, tell me, Ms. Corduroy. Chicks dig a poetic soul, right?"

"Milrose, in this progressive world, we do not have 'chicks.' And were we to have such creatures, they would not 'dig' anything."

"Right. I see your point. My question—if I may rephrase it—my question is . . . if I were, like, to develop a completely poetic soul—we're talking a serious, hardcore rhyming sensibility—you think I'd be able to land a serious babe?"

"Milrose, the words 'serious babe' are not . . ." She sighed. Caroline Corduroy was clearly giving up in her efforts to purge the Munce vocabulary. And, now that he had a quasi-poetic soul, she no longer felt a pressing urge to do so. "Yes, I believe that a poetic soul is an aid in the pursuit of romance."

"Hot damn," said Milrose. "Time to crack open that Virgil!"

"Damnation is indeed hot," said Ms. Corduroy. "I suggest you ponder that as you advance through life."

Milrose, who ignored this, became silent and thoughtful. He had not had a conversation about romance with Caroline Corduroy for some time. In fact, not since that fateful detention. In further fact, he had only ever had one, and it had not gone well.

"Um, Ms. Corduroy?"

"Yes, Milrose."

"I . . . uh, I guess I have to make a confession."

"I am prepared, Milrose."

"Okay. Well, this is hard to say. And I really hope you won't be offended."

"I shall do my best."

"Right. Okay. Well. The problem . . . I mean, I feel bad about this . . . but, much as it used to dominate my every daydream . . . well, I no longer have the overwhelming desire to ponder your birthmark."

Principal Corduroy arched an eyebrow. "I think I can live with that, Milrose."

"Oh, good. I mean, I'm really sorry. It's just . . . well, I have another birthmark to think about now, and it just doesn't seem right . . . it doesn't seem *loyal*, somehow, to have promiscuous daydreams. Birthmark-wise."

"I am glad that you have come to this highly ethical conclusion." She began to arrange the papers on her desk. "And now, Milrose Munce, I think it is time to return to more serious matters than the discussion of frivolous matters with you."

"Right. See you, Principal Corduroy. Have a good one. Ta-ta."

As Milrose sauntered jauntily out the door, Caroline Corduroy, in spite of herself, felt a moment's sadness, and lightly touched the birthmark on the side of her neck.

"Mom, can I ask you something?"

Mrs. Munce was on a ladder, spraying a corner of the ceiling that had recently proved a favourite hangout for a posse of tiny flesh-eating ants. "Certainly, dear."

"Why *did* you call me Milrose? And whatever got into you to saddle me with Bysshe?"

"Oh, that."

"Yes, that."

"Well . . ." Mrs. Munce shook the can, which had blocked up, and then gave a good squirt into the corner. "Are you sure you want to know?"

"Is it something that's going to upset me?"

"No. I just wanted to make sure that you were sure you wanted to know."

"Uh, yeah. I'm sure. That's why I asked the question."

"Okay." Mrs. Munce was finished with the ant prevention. "Could you take the poison, dear?"

"What do you mean by that?"

"I mean, could you hold this can of insecticide while I come down the ladder."

"Oh. Sure."

Milrose took the poison from her hand. "So . . ."

"What, dear?"

"So you were going to tell me why you called me Milrose Bysshe."

"Oh yes. Of course." Mrs. Munce was now folding the ladder closed. This took her some time. When the ladder was folded, she tipped it carefully and tucked it under her arm. It was light, but difficult to balance, and required all of her concentration for a moment.

"Well . . . we decided to call you Milrose Bysshe Munce, so that we could be certain when you had grown up to be an intelligent and inquisitive young man." She paused. "Because then you would approach one of us and ask: 'Why did you call me Milrose Bysshe?'"

"That's *it*?"

"I'm afraid so, dear."

The grass in front of the school was in much better shape now that Ms. Corduroy had taken control of things. "It is not acceptable," Ms. Corduroy had said to the new gardener, "that the grass be greener on the other side. It must be greener on *this* side." And so it was.

Milrose Munce and Arabella sat on the healthy grass, and enjoyed a bowl of jungerberries, which were currently in season and very, very good. Arabella's flower, which was lovelier than ever and feeling magnificent, stretched and yawned in the sun.

"I have an announcement to make," said Arabella, who was looking unnaturally cheerful. Arabella, although often happy these days, took care not to show it, as this would put a dent in her pretense.

"Do announce," said Milrose, who was made happy by Arabella's happiness.

"I have new parents."

"You what?"

"I have an entire new set of parents. A matched set."

"Congratulations! How did you manage that?"

"The DNA tests came back. They came back negative."

"Which means?"

"Which means that the dull and inhospitable people who I thought were my parents—and who thought I was in need of Professional Help—are not my parents at all. It seems there was a mix-up at the hospital. *Their* child is in fact an incredibly dim and boring girl who is hoping to major in economics."

"This is wonderful news."

"Yes, it is, isn't it."

"So who are the new guys?"

"Well, my actual parents, whom I met for dinner last night, are very much . . . the kind of people who should have given birth to me."

"As they should be. Since they did."

"I hadn't thought of that. You are quite right."

"So tell me about them."

"My real father," said Arabella with unconcealed pride, "is an experimental bassoonist."

"That's . . . so great."

"And my mother is a veterinarian who specializes in vampire bats."

"Gosh."

"And she moonlights as a radical theologian."

"Gosh squared."

"They seem to like me rather a lot."

Arabella, who never smiled, smiled.

"That's entirely the right thing to do. Like you rather a lot. I mean, I can't imagine anybody *sane* who wouldn't like you rather a huge serious ton, in fact."

At which point Milrose Munce stopped, both flushing and blushing, for once again his mouth had raced so far ahead of him that it was a mere pink blip on the horizon. "I didn't mean that."

Arabella tried to hide her disappointment.

"I mean I didn't mean to *say* that."

Arabella tried to hide her confusion.

"I mean, the meaning of what I meant was very meaningful. To me. Entirely meaningful. I've never meant anything more sincerely in my life. I just didn't mean to, like, well, I didn't mean to . . ."

"Declare it?"

"Precisely. Couldn't have put it better myself. That's what I meant. Precisely what I meant. Meaning couldn't be any clearer than that."

"You can stop speaking now, Milrose Munce."

"I can?"

"Yes. Have a jungerberry."

"Thank you."

"And that was an act of speech."

"Sorry."

They sat in silence.

"My real name," she finally said, "turns out to be Arabella Asquith the Third."

"I'm so *happy* for you."

"Thank you, Milrose."

Arabella slipped her hand into his. And the world, astonishingly, did not crack in half and spill its molten yolk.

"Arabella?"

"Yes, Milrose?"

"May I ask you something?"

"Of course."

"Um, Arabella? Do you . . . have a birthmark, by any chance?"

"In fact," said Arabella, "I do not."

THE END

DOUGLAS ANTHONY COOPER is an evil novelist. He has written two depressing books for adults: *Amnesia* and *Delirium*. Critics like his novels, but Cooper himself is widely loathed, and has to switch cities every few months. His gloomy magazine articles have won America's top travel writing award—the Lowell Thomas Gold Medal—as well as a Canadian National Magazine Award. He was last spotted in Mexico.